BOLD AS BRASS

She didn't really want to shoot him, just impress upon him that he couldn't trifle with her. The pistol suddenly felt very heavy in Rosalind's hand, her fingers itchy and nervous. Her outstretched arm wobbled and dipped as her muscles ached. The tip of the little gun wavered in the air, frightening Rosalind as much as the viscount.

He looked at the pistol, then at her. "Now, don't get excited. Why don't you simply hand me the gun?"

"I-I can't do that."

"Yes, you can. No harm done. Would you mind not pointing that thing at my chest?"

He wasn't afraid of her, she saw that. But, she also saw the tremendous respect he had for the gun that quivered in her hand. Her courage returned, and she thought it was only fair that after he'd overpowered her and kidnapped her, she should suddenly have the upper hand. "I don't want to have to shoot you," she told him, clasping the stock of the pistol now with both hands. "Do as I say and I won't hurt you. I promise."

His lips curled, but he lifted his hands in surrender. "Alright, you're in control. What is it that you'd have me do?"

She thought about the moment on the beach, when she'd lifted her face to be kissed by him. A sinful impulse overtook her. "Kiss me."

BOOK YOUR PLACE ON OUR WEBSITE AND MAKE THE READING CONNECTION!

We've created a customized website just for our very special readers, where you can get the inside scoop on everything that's going on with Zebra, Pinnacle and Kensington books.

When you come online, you'll have the exciting opportunity to:

- View covers of upcoming books
- Read sample chapters
- Learn about our future publishing schedule (listed by publication month *and author*)
- Find out when your favorite authors will be visiting a city near you
- Search for and order backlist books from our online catalog
- Check out author bios and background information
- Send e-mail to your favorite authors
- Meet the Kensington staff online
- Join us in weekly chats with authors, readers and other guests
- Get writing guidelines
- AND MUCH MORE!

Visit our website at
http://www.zebrabooks.com

THE
SMUGGLER'S
BRIDE

Bess Willingham

ZEBRA BOOKS
Kensington Publishing Corp.
http://www.zebrabooks.com

This book is for BVS

ZEBRA BOOKS are published by

Kensington Publishing Corp.
850 Third Avenue
New York, NY 10022

Copyright © 2000 by Cindy Harris-Williams

Zebra and the Z logo Reg. U.S. Pat. & TM Off.

First Printing: September, 2000
10 9 8 7 6 5 4 3 2 1

Printed in the United States of America

One

Bonfires, strung like diamonds on a necklace, lit a quarter mile of the coastline. It seemed everyone in Hastings, and perhaps Brighton and Rye as well, had come to celebrate Guy Fawkes Day on this particular stretch of sandy beach. Against the starless night sky, fires sizzled as the heavy oaken timbers supporting them crackled and shifted. A pleasant smokiness prickled at Miss Rosalind Yardley's nose. But, as usual, despite the jolly mood surrounding her, she was bored.

"Don't wander off without your governess, dear. The carriages will soon be returning to Brighton!" Lady Dovie Yardley's voice was as bright as her lime-green suit, and as sprightly as her trim figure. Cheeks apple-tinted from the heat of the bonfires, she glowed with youthful vigor. Hardly a maternal figure. "And where is Mrs. Childress, anyway?"

Rosalind forced a practiced smile to her lips. "She's just gone to the carriage to get a warmer wrap. If you don't mind, I think I'll go and join her." Then, when her stepmother and her father had turned their backs, Rosalind headed toward the steep path that led to the beach, a crudely carved set of stairs leading from the ridge overlooking the ocean to the wall of caverns below.

She'd learned well the art of nodding and smiling at her father and stepmother, feigning agreement with everything they said or suggested. But, lately she'd fallen into the habit of doing precisely as she pleased, in total disregard of what they wanted.

They were, after all, completely preoccupied with each other and their own lives. They didn't understand Rosalind or the way she felt. They loved her— yes, she was quite sure her father at least loved her—but they didn't have time to get to know her. She considered her stepmother dull and vapid, her father exquisitely naive. And she ached for the day when she was free from their control, free from the restrictions they imposed upon her.

The Guy Fawkes celebration on the oceanfront ledge was a perfect example of her stepmother's silly impulsiveness. Why Hastings? Why not Brighton, where her father maintained a fabulously sumptuous town house? And, why for heaven's sake, on the spur of the moment, and on a starless, moonless, pitch-black night when no one but smugglers, thieves, and brigands had any business being out on the road?

Because I'm sick of Brighton, darling, her stepmother doubtless had cooed into Sir Sibbald Yardley's ear. *And because it would be so jolly to surprise our friends by loading them into a caravan of carriages and setting off for Hastings beach.*

And so, the second Battle of Hastings had ensued,

during which Sir Sibbald Yardley argued in vain, while his manservant was attempting to tie his cravat, that their dinner party would be ruined by the announcement of a late night trek to Hastings. Whereupon Lady Dovie Yardley, her back as straight as a poker, her head as still as a statue while her abigail combed and plaited and piled her hair atop her head, returned that if she wasn't allowed to take her dinner guests to Hastings for the bonfires, she would surely have the megrims and would be required to take to her bed—quite alone, thank you—for an indefinite period of recovery.

In the end, of course, the Hastings expedition was announced with great gaiety by Sir Sibbald as the Yardleys' dinner guests ate their floating islands of meringue. And by the time the caravan of four carriages and two riders on horseback made it to the Hastings beach, the Sibbald servants, who'd spent the afternoon building them, had managed to construct half a dozen huge bonfires, paced at equidistant intervals along the coastal ridge.

Descending the steps to the beach, Rosalind shuddered as much from the thought of her stepmother's frivolity and her father's doting indulgence as the chilly breeze that sliced through her. Standing near the bonfires, she'd been cozy and warm. By the time she made it to the sandy shore, coldness had burrowed beneath her ermine-lined cloak and seeped straight through to her gooseflesh.

A tinkle of feminine laughter, recognizable as Lady Dovie Yardley's, carried on the night air. The sound sent another little shiver through Rosalind, a sensation that had nothing to do with the sudden drop in temperature or the quick increase in the dampness that surrounded her.

Oh, she just had to get away from that horrible, horrible woman, that woman who had stolen her father from her and . . . well, yes, ruined Rosalind's life. If she didn't escape Lady Dovie Yardley's silvery laugh and perfect smile for just one minute, she thought she'd wind up throttling the woman. She had to get away, find a place to be alone for a moment and collect her thoughts. Trudging through the wet sand, water lapping at her leather half-boots, she just wanted to get away. She just wanted to be *alone*.

Wind lashed her skirts about her legs and disheveled her upswept coiffure. Rosalind felt the spray of the ocean on her cheeks, and tasted salt on her lips. Down here, the bonfires were mere candle-bursts of flame on the ridge above. The chatter of Dovie's friends was drowned by the crash of the waves on the beach. Viewing the festive scene from a distance, Rosalind could almost pretend her father had never married Lady Dovie.

A flash of blue light on the ocean's surface drew her attention. Stock still, Rosalind peered into the void. In the darkness, nothing but streaks of frothy white, the cusps of waves pounding the shoals, appeared.

Another light flashed in the corner of her eye, and she turned completely around. This one seemed to have come from the ridge, behind the bonfires, perhaps in one of the windows of the tall, shingled net house that stored the fishermen's tackle.

Wrapping her cloak more tightly around her, Rosalind stared down the beach, toward the headland and the jutting shoreline. Against the night sky, nothing but the dim limning of the rocky cave was visible. But, she knew the cavern well from her girlhood visits to Hastings, when her mother used to bring her here to play in the surf and picnic on the ledge. Stories of ancient mariners stranded on the shoals came to Rosalind's mind. Her mother had been a wonderful storyteller; the times they'd spent wandering the beaches between Brighton and Rye were some of Rosalind's most treasured memories.

She missed her mother.

Glancing at the bonfires above her, Rosalind marched toward the black cave, drawn by some irresistible force. On the other side was another stretch of sandy beach, not so heavily strewn with rocky shoals, but a dangerous shoreline for local fishermen nevertheless. Only the local men with intimate knowledge of the tides could safely navigate these treacherous waters.

Many a time Rosalind and her mother had seen bits of jetsam, broken timbers, bales of contraband tobacco, and pieces of hogsheads, tubs and ankers, washed ashore by the vicious waves. Even then, the thought of what hadn't washed ashore, what lay at the bottom of the ocean, never to be found or rescued, had set Rosalind's imagination spinning.

She knew her father would have apoplexy if he knew what she was about. And Lady Dovie Yardley would have a fit of the vapors, or at least fake one. But, Rosalind couldn't stop herself. She bent against the slicing wind as if she were being poured out of a ewer, and stalked toward that cavern as if she were being spilled into it. The wet, earthy smell of the cave filled her nostrils even before she found the opening. The icy chill of the cold, rocky walls rippled through her even before her shoes slipped on the wet, rubbled entrance.

One last glance over her shoulder . . . the fires burned brightly. Mrs. Childress was no doubt hidden behind a carriage sipping from her flask. Dovie wouldn't notice Rosalind's absence for a while, and Sir Sibbald was so absorbed with Dovie he wouldn't miss his daughter for a sennight. Entering the cave, a delicious rebelliousness welled up inside Rosalind. Blackness engulfed her, and she stilled, uncertain of her footing.

She closed her eyes, content to stand there, remembering her mother's stories, reliving the carefree summers of her childhood when exploring this cave was a great adventure, when her mother was well and happy and her father was . . . well, when her father was her father and not the stranger who had married Miss Dovie, the buxom blonde from Brighton who wouldn't have set foot on a sandy beach or inside a cave if her life depended on it, not if it meant getting the hem of her skirts wet, or the soles of her pretty satin slippers soiled.

A quick rasping sound cut through her reverie. Rosalind's eyes flew open. Another flash of light, this a small yellow one, was followed by a flame that seemed to float in the air. My God, was there a ghost in the cave? If her legs hadn't been frozen in fear,

Rosalind would have turned and hightailed it back to the beach, back to the stairs, back to the ridge and the safety of Dovie's horrid party. But, the fear that seized her also paralyzed her. She gasped, clutching at her cloak, staring openmouthed at the flame that floated toward her.

"Crawley? The devil man, you're late!" The masculine voice, deep and menacing, was also pleasantly refined.

She took a step back as the man's face came into view.

"Damme, you're not Crawley. Who are you? And what the hell are you doing here?"

"I was on the ridge, at the party . . . with my parents," Rosalind stammered, squinting to see past the glaring light.

He stepped closer, holding the lantern so that his face, albeit bathed in shadow, was clearly visible. "For God's sake, what sort of fool would throw a party on this deserted stretch of beach?"

"My stepmother," Rosalind replied. "She and her friends are celebrating Guy Fawkes Day."

With his free hand, he pinched the bridge of his nose. *His very straight, very handsome nose.* Rosalind studied the man more closely, noting the snug breeches that outlined his muscular thighs, and the long leather boots that emphasized his lean legs. No, this definitely was not the ancient mariner her mother had told her about. This man, with his thick black hair and his piercing black eyes, had the air of a pirate, true, but his fine lawn shirt, open at the neck, and his elegantly cut wool coat, bespoke a man of culture, taste, and wealth. Frankly put, he was a portrait rife with contradiction.

Behind him, past the opening that led to the eastern side of the beach, a great ruckus reached Rosalind's ears. She strained to see, but the stranger shifted and blocked her view.

"Are you on the beach alone?"

She met his gaze. "Yes. No. Well, my father will miss me shortly, if you are thinking to—"

"I'm not thinking to harm you, gel!" His voice held a note of irritation. "You've wandered somewhere you shouldn't be, though, I'll tell you that bloody much."

"I'll thank you not to use such vulgarities in my presence." Rosalind, her cheeks stinging, turned on her heel. She'd not suffer this rogue talking that way to her! Why, her father would pistol-whip a man for speaking so obscenely in the presence of a lady.

Lifting her skirts, she plunged toward the cave's opening. The stranger's lantern cast an eerie glow over the rocky interior of the cavern, and his sinister chuckle frightened her. Suddenly, she craved the company of Dovie's silly friends and the warm embrace of her father. She'd been foolish to wander off alone. If the stranger attacked her, if she screamed, no one would hear her.

Aware of her vulnerability, she felt a surge of panic. Behind her, the stranger called out, "Hurry, get out of here!" And her fear increased. Heart thudding, she plunged over the slippery rocks. Until she fell. Head over heels. And landed with a painful thud on a pile of rubble and flotsam.

The stranger cursed colorfully, and muttered, "Too late."

Her fear turned into certain dread. The noise Rosalind had heard on the eastern side of the beach, behind the stranger, gave way to the splash of booted footsteps. Twisting, she saw another man entering the cavern. Even in the dim light, Rosalind saw the cruel slash of the man's features, the glint of a gold loop in his earlobe, and the roughness of his manner.

Clad in a blue jacket, loose trousers and a white cap, he was precisely what Rosalind expected a salty mariner to look like. Which hardly gave her any comfort, for when he spied her, he halted, held up his torchlight and let loose his own stream of invectives. Rosalind hadn't heard so many curse words in her life as she'd heard in the last five minutes.

She started to stand, but pain shot through her hip and down her leg. Behind her, the men spoke in hushed tones. Frozen, she struggled to make out their words.

After a moment, the handsome stranger's voice grew louder. "She hasn't seen a thing, damn it."

The sailor replied, "She's seen you, ain't she? That's enough, I'm tellin' ye."

"Get back to the gang, Jemmy—"

"You've told her me name, now!"

"She's harmless, man. Do you really want to get yourself in trouble? Harm some wealthy gentry man's daughter, and you'll have everybody from the excise man to the local magistrate to the parish vicar breathing down your neck! Do you want that, Jemmy? I didn't think so. Now, go! Get back to work. There's another dozen barrels of wine to off-load, and fifty more ankers of brandy.''

"I'll be damned." The sailor turned his head and spat, gave Rosalind one last angry look, then left.

The cave grew colder. As the realization of what she'd stumbled onto crept into her conscious mind, Rosalind's terror grew. Smugglers were notoriously cutthroat. She should know. Her father had made it his life's work to rid this area of them.

Wobbling like a colt, she stood. She had to get out of that cavern, had to make it back to the beach and then to the ridge. God, where was the noisy Dovie when Rosalind needed her? Where was her father? Where were the revenue men who were supposed to patrol this stretch of shoreline?

"You're not going anywhere. Not for the moment, anyway." The stranger's voice echoed off the walls of the cave.

She bolted for the cave's western aperture, but the stranger was quicker than she. And her body ached in places she hadn't known existed. Effortlessly, he overtook her, clasping her arm and turning her to face him. She felt his fingers through the woolen cloak and she was appalled by the strength in his grip.

Not looking at him, she said, "Please, sir. Let me go. I haven't even seen your face. I couldn't describe you if I had I to."

"You never told me your name."

Good heavens, she wasn't going to now! Any smuggler worth his salt would recognize the name Yardley, would know that he'd captured the daughter of the magistrate, the most rabid antismuggling government official in Sussex.

"You don't need to know my name. I don't know yours. Why don't we simply leave it at that?" Rosalind tried to retreat, but the stranger's fingers were like an iron band around her upper arm.

"I'm afraid it's not quite that simple." He pulled her along with him as he walked toward the cave's opposite entrance. "We need to have a little talk. Come with me."

She stumbled, and he paused. "Are you hurt?"

"I believe I twisted my ankle," she lied, hoping that if he thought she was injured, he might spare her.

Spare her from what? She had only the vaguest notion of the potential harm he might do her, but it was enough to set her heart thudding. Hoping to convince him that she was no threat to his smuggling operation, she looked into his black gaze, and said, "Just leave me, sir. I won't tell a soul, you can trust me."

His dark stare was skeptical. "The last time I trusted a woman . . ."

"Yes?" Her arm slipped out of his fingers, but she didn't move. She should have pivoted and run for the beach, for safety and the cold comfort of her family's protection. Instead, she stood there gazing at this handsome stranger, clearly a smuggler, the very sort of outlaw her father would have tossed into gaol without blinking an eye.

It seemed very wicked to be talking to him. "The last time you trusted a woman . . . what?"

He closed his eyes and let out a harsh breath. When he opened them, Rosalind thought she saw the sparkle of a tear, but it mustn't have been, for his jaw was as hard as stone. "Upon reflection, a talk wouldn't do a whit of good. Get out of here," he said in a low, gravelly voice. "Get out of here, and don't ever tell anyone that you saw a soul on this godforsaken beach. Do you hear me?"

"Yes. Yes, I promise." She had enough sense to realize her luck. Yet, her slippers were planted to the ground.

He grasped her arm again, squeezing her muscle through the thick wool of her cloak. "I said go, damn it!"

"You curse too much. It isn't polite." Rosalind stepped closer to him. Rebellion raced through her. It was so naughty to be talking to a man her father would have arrested on the spot. It was so scandalous to be *alone* in this wet, dark cavern, flirting so outrageously with a mysterious, possibly dangerous stranger. She pictured Lady Dovie swooning. Then, she lifted her face, closed her eyes, parted her lips and waited for the stranger to kiss her.

As the seconds ticked by, Rosalind's body thrummed with excitement. But, her excitement turned to disappointment, and disappointment turned to embarrassment when he didn't kiss her. As the moment stretched longer, Rosalind waited, her cheeks growing ever warmer, her feet colder. Why didn't he kiss her? Was she too brazen? Too bold? Even for this rough-and-tumble criminal?

Her eyes flung open. Hateful cad! How dare he

not kiss her! She was angry now, and she felt like slapping him. Drawing back her hand, she froze. The handsome smuggler wasn't even looking at her. Something else had snagged his attention. Something had darkened his expression so that Rosalind's own anger suddenly turned to fear.

The splash of another footstep sounded, this time from the western entrance. Was it one of his men, gone around the other side of the cavern for some inexplicable reason? Lifting his lantern, Rafe strained to see who had entered the cave. Perhaps one of the girl's party had followed her. Christ on a raft! Was he about to meet the entire lot of them?

The footsteps approached, heavy and deliberate. Instinctively, Rafe reached for the girl, pulling her behind him. His own men would have identified themselves. If this were someone looking for the girl, why didn't they call out her name? What the devil was her name, by the way?

Reaching behind him, he pulled a small pistol from the waistband of his breeches. He was startled, and somewhat irritated, to feel the girl's body pressed against his, her arms going round his middle as if she were holding onto him for protection. What a little fool she was, not even smart enough to be afraid of him!

The interloper slowly stepped into the penumbra of lantern light. When his face came into view, Rafe pulled back the hammer of his pistol. The appearance of Cyril Crawley, the revenue man responsible for this stretch of beach, complicated matters greatly.

"Enjoying the bonfires, Lord Pershing?"

"I always enjoy Guy Fawkes day, Cyril. You know what a patriot I am."

The fat man, his face red from the cold, laughed heartily. "Aye, and what a fine group of friends to be spending this holiday with! Didn't get a gander at everyone up there on the ridge, but I sure as hell spotted Sir Sibbald Yardley and his wife. Didn't know you was an acquaintance of the magistrate. Socialize with him often, do you?"

"Yardley?" Rafe's fingers tightened on the pistol grip. "Is that who is up there?"

Mr. Crawley seemingly ignored the gun. "Who's the filly, Rafe?"

The girl's tiny breasts were crushed against his back. Her arms were wound so tightly about him that Rafe could hardly breathe. He felt her cheek pressed to his shoulder blade. She was afraid, and for some bizarre reason, he felt the urge to protect her from Cyril Crawley. "No one you know, Crawley. Now, why don't you be a good revenue man, and disappear? You'll be paid your usual cut, you know. No use in hanging around here, you'll only make my men nervous."

"I said, who's the girl?"

"Bad enough that you stick your nose in my import business. My women are none of your concern." Rafe pointed the gun at Cyril's heart, but it was an empty gesture. Shooting a revenue man would only bring unwanted attention to the smuggling operation. Both men knew that Rafe would never do it.

"Well, I hope it's not the Yardley chit. For God's sake, Rafe, if you've nabbed that child—"

"Bloody hell, man! Do I look like a kidnapper to you?"

"If it's the Yardley girl, you're in a heap of trouble, Rafe. Now let me see her, let me see her face!"

With the lantern in one hand, and his gun in the other, Rafe could do nothing but stand resolute. "No, Cyril. The woman has a reputation to be concerned about. To be caught alone with a rakehell like me in this cave would be ruinous to her good name. I won't allow you to humiliate her. I'll shoot you first, no matter the danger to my operation."

Cyril chuckled. "An odd code of chivalry you have there, Rafe, but I've got to admire you for it. You'd break every law in the country and risk life and limb to bring over that contraband whiskey and wine of yours. But, you'd kill a man for besmirching the honor of the woman you love? It's a trifle hard to swallow, old man."

"Who said anything about love?" Rafe snorted in derision. "However you put it, I'm not going to allow you to humiliate her."

"I don't believe you." Cyril's eyes narrowed. "I think it's the Yardley chit, and you've taken her against her will. Perhaps to extort favorable treatment from her father. Show me her face!"

"She's not the Yardley girl, and she's not with the Yardley party. If you must know, she's a married woman who's fled her husband, left him sleeping in his bed in Brighton. You've badly frightened her, and if she doesn't want to show her face, I won't make her."

"She's no married woman on the lam, she's Rosalind Yardley, the most overprotected child in Brighton. Lay a finger on that gel and you'll hang for it. Now let me see her!"

"No!" For an instant, Rafe thought he was going to have to shoot the revenue man, after all. Then, something happened that he would never have expected. The girl's hand slid from his middle down to the waist of his breeches. Slowly. Sinuously. Cyril gaped. Both men were speechless.

But, Rafe's reaction was complete and utter shock. When the girl's fingers toyed with the buttons on the opening of his breeches, he stopped breathing. A flood of heat roiled through his body. Carefully, he moved his finger from the trigger-guard of his pistol, and shoved it beneath the back waistband of his breeches, lest he accidently flinch and kill the revenue man by accident.

"Well . . ." Cyril licked his lips. "Perhaps I was wrong. Yardley's daughter is too well-bred for such tomfoolery."

"You were dead wrong," croaked Rafe. "Now get out of here."

The revenue man took a step backward, his eyes pinned to the feminine fingers dipping provocatively beneath the front waistband of Rafe's breeches. "I'll expect my usual cut."

"I told you, you'll get it. At the usual drop."

"I'll be going then. Perhaps I'll drop in on the Yardley bonfire party."

"That's a capital idea, Crawley. Good night, now."

As the revenue man splashed toward the western side of the cavern, Rafe turned and stared down at the girl. "What in God's name were you doing?" he whispered fiercely.

"I had to convince him I was no innocent child." She smiled up at Rafe, her eyes sparkling, her fingers walking along the open collar of his shirt.

For an instant, he thought of calling her bluff, taking her right then and there, in the shallow waters or against a flat rock. But, if she was Sibbald Yardley's daughter, and he was quite certain she was, she was more dangerous than a keg of gunpowder with a lit fuse. Tamping down his arousal, Rafe batted her hands from his chest. Then, he clasped her upper arm and shoved her toward the eastern entrance of the cavern.

They emerged onto the beach just as Jemmy and his cohorts, half a dozen Hastings ruffians who made their living on the wrong side of the law, loaded the last pallet of wine caskets to be conveyed up the side of the cliff. Dousing his lantern, Rafe stood still for a moment, allowing his eyes to adjust to the near blackness. Slowly, the dim silhouettes of men moving about the beachfront became visible.

"I can't see a thing!" the girl hissed. "Where's the ship?"

"Anchored a half-mile off the coast," Rafe replied. "The shallow waters are too treacherous for a big ship to anchor any closer. We offload the goods onto tiny fishing boats, then hire local men to row them ashore."

"And how are they going to get it from the beach to the ridge?"

"You ask too many questions, girl. You'll keep your mouth shut if you know what's good for you." Still clasping the girl's arm, Rafe led her toward a group of men at the base of the sheer cliff. The scene was dimly lit by a flickering *touchier*, strategically held against the wall of the cliff so as not to be visible from the top of the ledge.

As they approached, Rafe heard one of the men complaining bitterly that several of the French oak barrels had leaked and were now empty.

"Haul 'em up anyway," Jemmy said. "We don't want to leave any evidence of our bein' here on the beach." Turning away from the other men, Pratt gave Rafe and the girl a nasty appraisal. "What the devil is she doing here?"

Rafe held her close to his side. "Crawley wandered into the cave and accused me of kidnapping Sibbald Yardley's daughter. I had to pretend she was my . . . woman. Anyway, he didn't see her face."

"Sibbald Yardley's daughter? God's teeth, Pershing! If you're nabbed with that little minx in your possession, it won't go well for any of us. Get rid of her now, I tell you! I'll drown her in the ocean meself, if you ain't got the ballocks to do it!"

"You'll do no such thing, Pratt. We'll not add murder to our list of crimes. Besides, I'm not certain that she is—"

The girl twisted her arm free and pointed her finger at Pratt. "My father would hunt you down and slit your—"

Grabbing her elbow, Rafe gave her a little shake. The bad news was official: she was Sibbald Yardley's daughter. The thought made Rafe's hair bristle, but there was nothing to be done about it now. Nothing except get rid of her as quickly as possible. Not in the way Pratt had suggested, of course, but Rafe was going to have to think of something. And quickly.

"We've got to get this chit back to her family, Pratt."

"And what are we going to do when she blabs about having met a nice group of fellows on the beach, two of 'em named Pratt and Pershing, who just happened to be loading caskets of wine on a pallet and winching 'em up the side of the cliff? Think they'll say, 'Never mind about that, dear, we're just happy you're home?' "

Rafe realized his predicament. If the girl were harmed, he'd have Yardley, Crawley, the Brighton *ton*, and the entire coastal constabulary breathing down his neck. On the other hand, if he simply released the girl, she'd certainly tell her parents everything she'd heard and seen. This deserted little cove, which had been such a clever and well-hidden place to unload smuggled goods, would be overrun. Pratt and Pershing would be hunted down like common criminals. Crawley, once implicated, would sing like a bird, and Rafe's entire operation would come crashing down.

Anger knotted tightly in Rafe's gut. How the hell did this happen? How had he allowed one tiny little girl to threaten his livelihood, his freedom, his very reason for being?

"Christ on a raft," he muttered, flinging the unlit lantern on the ground, where it crashed and shattered against an outcropping of stone.

Some of the men rolling the last barrel onto the pallet paused, and looked at Rafe with interest. Their stares took in the entire scene, the pretty young girl included. As every moment passed, the girl observed more identifiable faces, and Jemmy grew more agitated. The situation was like a loaded cannon ready to explode.

"I strongly advise you, my lordship, to make that girl disappear!" Jemmy shifted his cheroot to the other side of his mouth, and propped his fists on his hips.

Make her disappear?

"Please." She nestled against Rafe's side, clutching at his arm. "Please don't let him kill me. I'll never tell, I swear it!"

Jemmy's laugh sent shivers of apprehension up and down Rafe's spine. The man would drown Sibbald Yardley's daughter like an unwanted kitten, if he had his way.

"Please." She was on her tiptoes, whispering in Rafe's ear. "I'll do anything . . . anything . . . just don't let that horrid man kill me!"

Just then, footsteps exploded from the cavern entrance. Rafe glanced over his shoulder in time to see Cyril Crawley trundling toward the base of the cliff. Holding his own torch aloft, the fat man's expression glowed with fear.

"She's not up there. I looked!" Crawley yelled between huffs. When he was a distance of some fifty yards, he paused, leaned over and heaved.

"A mite too fat to be runnin' like that," growled Jemmy. "Now what the 'ell are we goin' to do? There'll be a nervous papa and all his cronies swarming this beach 'ere long."

Rafe pushed the girl toward the loaded pallet. "Which one of those barrels is empty?" he demanded.

A brutish man wearing a striped shirt and baggy pants pointed to an oaken casket with a gaping hole in its side. "Reckon this one was dropped when it got put on at Calais."

"Open it!"

"What are you going to do with me?" The girl pulled against Rafe's grasp, but he easily picked her up in his arms and deposited her in the empty barrel. As Crawley's strangled cries grew louder, Rafe put his hand on top of the girl's head and pushed her down so that she was curled up in the barrel, hugging her knees. "Be quiet, and you'll come out of this in one piece. Make a sound, and I can't be responsible for what Mr. Pratt may do to you. He's a ruthless man, I'll warrant you."

She was silent as a church mouse as the ruffian replaced the barrel lid and gave the thumb's up signal to the men on the top of the ledge. The winch gears jolted into place, and the pallet slowly lifted off the ground. When Crawley stumbled onto the scene, the cargo was halfway up the side of the cliff. In a few minutes it would be off-loaded by the men above, transferred to a waiting mule-driven cart, and driven the short distance to Rafe's manor house in Rye.

"You're in a heap of trouble, Rafe. Where's the girl?" Crawley bent over double, attempting to catch his breath.

"What girl, Cyril?" Rafe clapped the fat man on the back, and gave Jemmy a wink. "Seen any girls around here, Pratt?"

"No girls," replied Jemmy. "A mermaid, perhaps. Mebbe even a siren, or two. But no girls."

Crawley slowly straightened, his face ruddy and sweat-soaked in the dim torch light. "God help you, Lord Pershing, if you've nabbed Sibbald Yardley's daughter."

"What makes you think the Yardley girl is even missing?" Rafe asked, glancing at the pallet inching its way upward.

Cyril ran his sleeve over his brow. "I asked everybody where she was. *'I haven't seen her, she must be over there,'* is what they all told me. Soon enough, they'll realize she's gone missin'. And there'll be hell to pay, my lord. I can't protect you this time."

"I don't expect you, to, Cyril. If anyone asks, you'll say you never saw a thing. Now say it, man. You never saw a thing!"

"I never saw a thing." Crawley shook his head. "Good luck, Rafe. You're in over your head this time."

"I'll second that." Jemmy Pratt spat on the wet sand.

Rafe pinched the bridge of his nose in a vain attempt to staunch the pain of his throbbing temples.

He was in over his head, he feared. But not for the reasons that Cyril Crawley and Jemmy Pratt feared. There was something about that girl that bothered him. Something about her that made him feel protective of her. Something that aroused him.

And somehow Rafe Lawless, Viscount Pershing, knew that getting rid of Sibbald Yardley's daughter wasn't going to be easy.

Two

"Are you alright? Can you stand up?"

"Get me out of here!" Grasping the man's hand, Rosalind allowed him to pull her to her feet. Standing inside the barrel, she looked around. "Where am I?"

"You're in my wine cellar, Miss Yardley, beneath my house, just outside of Rye. Sorry for the cold. I'll take you abovestairs as soon as the servants have retired for the night. It is Miss Yardley, is it not?"

He put his hands around her waist and lifted her over the side of the wine casket. Rosalind's arms wound around his neck and, just for an instant, she rested her head on his shoulder. He smelled very manly, a little like the ocean. And, when he deposited her on the ground, she found it difficult to release her hold on him.

Strangely, she wanted him to hold her in his arms a bit longer—even though he hadn't been kind to her at all, and she thought him the worst sort of brute she'd ever encountered.

"Are you alright?" His hand lingered on her shoulder, and the warmth in his gaze startled her.

"I'm freezing, actually." Rosalind's slippers were inadequate protection against the chill that seeped up from the stone floors. "Isn't there a fireplace in here?"

His expression sobered as he stepped away from her. "It's meant to be cold in here. And humid. Helps to preserve my collection of wine and brandy. Would you like a glass of wine? I was just about to fix a spigot in that barrel there."

Rosalind looked at the rows and rows of wine racks surrounding her. The low-ceiling room seemed to stretch the length of a Brighton city block. Candles in wall sconces cast a dim glow over the dusty bottles, uneven walls, and the man who stood staring at her.

"I suppose a sip of wine wouldn't harm anything." She watched him pull a cork stopper from the top of an oaken barrel. As he inserted the spigot, she couldn't help but notice his broad shoulders and fine, strong hands. He'd taken off his coat, and rolled up the sleeves of his lawn shirt. It was open at the throat, revealing a tuft of black curly hair and an expanse of bronzed skin. Dimly, she wondered how it was that an Englishmen had got so much sun this time of year. But, her thoughts were replaced by a tinge of pain as she took a step toward him. The journey from Hastings to Rye had been downright painful, and every muscle in her body cramped and ached.

He handed her a large, balloon-shaped glass, about a third filled with a deep purplish wine.

"My hips hurt. And my head hurts. You almost killed me, shoving me in that barrel and bouncing me all over the place! Why did you do that?"

He held his wine up to the light, tipping the glass this way and that. "Five minutes after Cyril Crawley appeared on the beach, your father and a small search party followed. Jemmy and his crew hid behind a mound of rubble and flotsam while my friend Tom Wickham and I persuaded Sir Sibbald we'd not seen hide nor hair of you."

"Father must be sick with worry!"

"Yes." The handsome stranger dipped his nose in the glass, inhaling. When he looked at her, he sighed, and Rosalind could have sworn he was half-drunk already on the smell of the wine alone. "I suspect he is. But, I'll have you home soon enough, don't worry."

"Don't worry? How can I not? *Who are you?*"

"Well, if you didn't hear my name, I'm not inclined to tell you."

"But I did hear your name. You're Rafe Lawless, Viscount Pershing. That much I know. What I don't know is who you really are. What kind of man are you? What do you intend to do with me?"

He closed his eyes and tilted the glass to his lips. He let the wine glide over his lips, then he held it in his mouth for a moment before swallowing. Apparently in deep contemplation, he stood silently. Rosalind stared at him, unable to dismiss her interest in his long, lean legs, clad in revealingly snug breeches, his fine leather boots that gave him the air of a pirate, and the open-collared shirt, so white against his darkened skin. He was, she concluded, devilishly handsome.

When he opened his eyes and looked at her, a flush of heat stole up her neck. Oddly, she was embarrassed, as if she'd spied the man experiencing something quite personal and erotic. A slow, fluid smile played at his mouth and his eyes held a feral gleam. "Drink up, Miss Yardley. The wine is excellent."

And it had turned his voice to velvet. Nervous, she took too large a gulp, and coughed. "Yes, it is good," she sputtered.

He smiled. "You're not an experienced drinker, I see. Well, at your age, perhaps that is a good thing."

"My age? I'm perfectly old enough to do whatever I please, Lord Pershing."

"Perhaps you are."

The viscount's hungry stare filled Rosalind with a sexual awareness. She'd let her cloak fall open when she took the wineglass from him, and the front of her very flimsy and low-cut gown showed. She knew she had a fine, creamy little bosom, for Lady Dovie had tried like the dickens to have her cover it up that evening. But Rosalind took a great measure of satisfaction in piquing her stepmother's jealousy, for she was quite certain the woman was deliriously envious of her. After all, the older woman was intensely competitive, demanding more of Sir Sibbald's attention than she deserved, taking the man away from Rosalind a little more each day.

So, wearing her dresses a little too low-cut was Rosalind's most recent innovation in her war to win back her father's attention and make Lady Dovie's life miserable into the bargain. She'd thought it such a clever idea before. She'd been more than a little pleased when her father's brows lifted as she came down the stairs and stepped into the sitting parlor. And now, as she felt the heat of Lord Pershing's interest, she gave herself a mental pat on the back. She'd given this arrogant pirate a little shock, she told herself. She'd proved to him that she was old enough to take a drink . . . or do whatever she pleased. She supposed she'd set him in his place.

Another sip of her wine emboldened her. Half-turning to the side, she allowed her cloak to fall open a bit wider. She poked her nose into the wineglass the way he had done and inhaled deeply, so that her pert little breasts expanded. Slanting him a flirtatious glance, she used her best cat purr voice, the one that she used when she wanted to wheedle a new gown or feathered bonnet out of her dear old daddy. "You haven't told me why you kidnapped me, my lord."

He hesitated, his gaze fixed on her. She thought he found her fascinating. "On the contrary, I *have* told you. It was because your father would have had me hung if I were found with you in my possession. I got you off the beach the only way I knew how. When your father appeared, Tom and I told him we hadn't seen you. So, the search party turned and headed down the beach toward Brighton, in the opposite direction."

"What are you going to do with me now?"

"Return you to your home, of course."

"When?" She poked out her bottom lip. She'd

practiced that before the mirror. It had a great effect on her father. "I want to go now."

The viscount took another slow, careful sip. "I'll take you home when I'm ready, Miss Yardley."

The sultry menace in his voice caused Rosalind's chest to tighten. Suddenly, there was no sparkle in the viscount's eye, only a dangerous gleam. There was no indulgent smile on his lips, just a cruel curl at the corners of his mouth. And there was no hint in his black gaze that he was fascinated or captivated or helpless against her charms. Indeed, he appeared quite impervious to her wiles. He drained the wine from his glass and poured himself some more, his expression turning increasingly somber, his demeanor more businesslike.

The realization that she was trapped, held captive by a dangerous outlaw, felt like an anchor dropping on Rosalind's head. Fear stole through the soles of her slippers and crept up her limbs. Draining her own wineglass, she clutched at the front of her cloak, pulling it over her exposed bosom, shivering at the thought of what this dangerous villain could, and might yet, do to her.

"I think you have had quite enough," the viscount said, taking her glass from her fingers.

The touch of his skin against hers sent a delicious, dangerous thrill through her. He put the two glasses on a rough plank table against the wall. Then, he held out his hand for her, as if beckoning her to follow.

She lifted her chin a notch and sent him a withering stare. He was a bossy, arrogant man and she didn't like him. She didn't like any man whom she couldn't wind around her little finger. It hurt her feelings that he seemed not to care a whit about her sensibilities, her cold feet, or her bosom. It made her angry with him.

Well, she'd get even with Rafe Lawless, Viscount Pershing. She saw the look of irritation that creased his brow. When he took a step closer, grasping her elbow, pulling her along beside him, she wrenched loose and planted her feet on the cold stone floor.

"Come now, don't give me any problems," he said, as if he were speaking to a slow child.

Perhaps it was that patronizing tone that sent her over the edge. Or perhaps it was fear, or the fact that she'd finally met a man totally unimpressed by her beauty and social position. That old anger that she'd nurtured in her heart for so many years suddenly bloomed. The hurt she'd felt the day her father took her on his knee and told her he intended to marry that awful Dovie. Hadn't Rosalind been a good daughter, sweet and doting? Why had her father needed the affections of someone else? Why had she been forced to share her father with another woman?

And now, here was this horribly handsome villain, whose very touch sent shivers up her spine, but whose gaze, boring into her, was full of nothing but impatience. She hated him, she realized with an exultant vehemence. She despised him. And, as soon as she told her father what he'd done to her, he'd wish he had been a trifle kinder to her. Yes, that was what she would do. She'd tell her father everything. And, then, the arrogant Lord Pershing would realize he'd ignored quite the wrong woman. Rosalind Yardley would get his attention, one way or the other, even if it meant seeing him in prison.

As his strong fingers closed around her upper arm, a surge of defiant courage poured through Rosalind's veins. "You're hurting me!" she cried, but stumbled along toward the crumbling stone staircase without any real resistance. After all, she had something in the inner pocket of her cloak that he was unaware of. She had the means of escaping him, and she knew how to use it. Her father would be proud when he heard how she so bravely freed herself from Lord Pershing's captivity. Dovie would swoon. People in Brighton would talk for years about her daring.

Oh, this would make a delicious story! Rosalind's hand slipped inside her cloak, and her fingers closed around the pearl-handled butt of the pistol she'd removed from Rafe's waistband. She allowed herself to be pushed up the narrow stairwell into the main house, emerging beside the viscount in a dark corridor. She had to wait until there was sufficient light, following Lord Pershing down the hall and up a wide carpeted staircase and into a dark, rather cold parlor. She was holding his hand now, perhaps more tightly than he was holding hers.

"Stand here, I'll light some candles." He moved about the room and the semidarkness faded into light as he brought tapers and sconces to life.

It was his favorite room in the house, a room where he and his wife had often spent the evenings before a great crackling fire, she with her needlepoint, he with a book. Rafe quickly built a fire, his back to

Rosalind Yardley, his mind muddled with thoughts of Annette. A fine Bordeaux often summoned thoughts of her, he mused, stoking the fire with an iron poker.

As warmth suffused the room, he stared into the flames. For a moment, he felt Annette in the room again. Her long, elegant fingers moving so deftly with the sewing needle. Her quiet smile. She'd been so beautiful when he married, so much more beautiful when she'd died. And, turning to face the young Rosalind Yardley, he thought his Annette had been so much like her, young and headstrong. The apple of her father's eye.

He recognized in Rosalind's expression a sort of girlish infatuation. She was very near the age Annette was when he met her. Sweet and impressionable, she hadn't yet sorted out all the emotions she felt for a man to whom she was attracted.

But, Rafe knew Rosalind's mind better than she did. He knew what she was about because he recalled Annette's wistful regret after they'd eloped to Gretna Green. She'd been too young, she'd murmured. . . .

Then, somewhere near the end, when honesty was all she had left, when her candor became the curse she bequeathed him, she confessed it all. She'd been too young, and she hadn't any notion of what *forever* had meant when she'd said, "I do."

The hurt of her admission still pained him. He'd taken a precious woman away from her family. For love and passion, the beautiful, elegant Annette had wed a man of inferior title and dubious future. She'd cheerfully married a man with the gall and coarseness to conduct a shipping enterprise, rather than spend his days buying horseflesh at Tattersall's and his nights playing faro at White's or Watier's.

The first two years it didn't matter. They had a joyous honeymoon. But soon enough Annette missed her father, and when she journeyed from Rye to London to reunite with him, she was disappointed to learn that his disapproval of her impulsive marriage hadn't dulled. Returning to Rye, she grew quieter than before. She said everything was alright, but increasingly she complained of the megrims, or fatigue, or shortness of breath.

Rafe should have taken her to London, then, should have found her the finest doctors and moved her away from Rye. But, she was young, sometimes petulant and immature, and too often, he underestimated the gravity of her physical complaints, or mistook them for ploys for his attention. He was so busy, after all, making his fortune in the shipping business. He'd thought it vitally important that he earn as much money as he could, that he become as wealthy as he could, so that he could someday provide for Annette the way her father had.

He didn't know whether he'd earned her respect, but he knew he hadn't earned her father's. On the day Annette died, the old duke had spat on Pershing's boots.

"My baby." His rheumy eyes narrow, the man had jabbed a gnarled finger at Rafe's chest. "You killed her."

Too overwhelmed by grief to reply, Rafe had merely shook his head. "I loved her."

"Yet you stuck her in this godforsaken corner of the earth, and let her die of boredom. 'Twas the sea air and your selfishness that killed her. Had you left her in London, with her friends and family and doctors, she'd be alive this day!"

The memory sent a shudder through Rafe's body. He closed his eyes, shutting it out, along with the increasingly troubling image of Rosalind Yardley, who stood on the opposite side of the room, staring at him with her pretty, round blue eyes.

Yes, she was pretty. Young enough to have the vulnerability of a child, and old enough to possess the allure of a temptress. And had Rafe not kidnapped her in order to prevent Cyril Crawley from identifying her, he would have been sorely tempted to kiss her. But, there was no question of the danger she posed to him now. He had to return her to her father before the man had a search party scouring the coast, invading every house between Brighton and Rye. He had to get her out of his house, and out of his hair.

Most of all, he had to get rid of the memory of her soft little breasts pressed against his back.

He heard her slippers pad across the thick Axminster carpet. Opening his eyes, he saw that she was an arm's length away from him. Her blue eyes were large and liquid beneath perfectly shaped black brows. Her lashes were thick black fringes that reminded him of the silk tips of painting brushes. Her pretty bow-shaped lips were slightly parted and still glistening with the stain of red wine.

His mouth watered for the taste of that wine on

her lips. His body hungered for the feel of Rosalind Yardley in his arms again.

Suddenly, his muscles froze as his gaze lowered to the shiny pistol she gripped in her hands. His pistol. The one he'd tucked beneath the waistband of his pants at the small of his back. Clever minx. A part of him couldn't help but be impressed by her courage and ingenuity. Yes, she had the sort of spirited defiance he liked in a woman.

He only hoped she knew how to handle a pistol. Being accidentally shot in the heart would certainly take the fun out of tangling with this saucy little tigress.

She didn't really want to shoot him, just impress upon him that he couldn't trifle with her. The pistol suddenly felt very heavy in Rosalind's hand, her fingers itchy and nervous. Her outstretched arm wobbled and dipped as her muscles ached. The tip of the little gun wavered in the air, frightening Rosalind as much as the viscount.

He looked at the pistol, then at her. "Now, don't get excited. Why don't you simply hand me the gun?"

"I-I can't do that."

"Yes, you can. No harm done. Would you mind not pointing that thing at my chest?"

He wasn't afraid of her, she saw that. But, she also saw the tremendous respect he had for the gun that quivered in her hand. Her courage returned, and she thought it was only fair that after he'd overpowered her and kidnapped her, she should suddenly have the upper hand. "I don't want to have to shoot you," she told him, clasping the stock of the pistol now with both hands. "Do as I say and I won't hurt you. I promise."

His lips curled, but he lifted his hands in surrender. "Alright, you're in control. What is it that you'd have me do?"

She thought about the moment on the beach, when she'd lifted her face to be kissed by him. A sinful impulse overtook her. "Kiss me."

"Did I hear correctly? You want me to kiss you?"

"You want it, too. I'm aware of that, you see. You'd have kissed me in the cavern if you hadn't been afraid of being arrested."

He tilted his head. "You know a lot about men, do you?"

"I'm not as young as you may think."

His hands lowered a bit and she waved the pistol about. Quickly, he thrust them back in the air. "Precisely how old *are* you?"

"Twenty-two." She couldn't resist a laugh. "My stepmother Dovie thinks I'm on the shelf. I've been through three London seasons, and I've yet to find a man who interested me. What do you think of that?"

He grinned. "You are quite old, aren't you? 'Struth, I'd have guessed you were seventeen at the most. But, twenty-two! Why, I suspect you've had a world of experience with men by now. Have you ever kissed one?"

He was mocking her, and she thought that was a very foolish thing for him to do under the circumstances. Behind her, in the corridor outside the parlor, she heard a floorboard squeak. She threw a glance over her shoulder, but saw nothing in the dark hallway. When she looked back at Viscount Pershing, his gaze had lit on the snout of her pistol, but he hadn't moved an inch.

"Who else is in the house?" she asked, retreating just a step.

"The servants are all abed. Of course, if you shoot me, I'm certain you'll awaken the entire household."

"Kiss me, and I won't shoot you."

"And how am I to kiss you, dear girl, while there is a loaded firearm between us? Don't you think you should toss it down, so that I can ravish you properly?"

"You think you can trick me." Scanning the room, Rosalind jerked her pistol toward a crimson velvet covered sofa. She directed the viscount toward it with a wave of her pistol, and—still with his hands in the air—he slowly complied. "Sit down, now. Yes, that's it. Hands up in the air! I won't have you snatching the pistol from me."

Switching the gun from one hand to the other, she managed to remove her heavy cloak. When her back was to the parlor door, she stood before him in her flimsy empire-waist gown, the one that her father had nearly made her change out of when she'd descended the stairs to dinner earlier that night.

The viscount's gaze roved the length of her body, and that, coupled with the heat from the crackling fire he'd built, warmed her bare shoulders and neck. Her bosom swelled quite involuntarily as he looked

at her, and a gush of liquid heat fanned through her
limbs. Another board behind her creaked, and she
looked around again, very quickly, for her attention
was riveted to the viscount's hungry expression.

"It's an old house," he said, his voice thick and
deep. "When the wind blows, it sounds as if it's groan-
ing."

She took a deep breath. Her heart pounded so
loudly now that she could hardly hear anything above
it. She stared at the viscount, his long booted legs
slightly parted, his fine elegant hands slowly lowering
to the sofa cushions.

"Well, if you're going to kiss me, get on with it,"
he said.

Her nerves were drawn tight as a bow. She didn't
dare let go of the pistol, but she transferred it to one
hand while she considered how she should go about
having her way with Rafe Lawless, Viscount Pershing.
Should she step between his lean, muscular legs,
bend down and kiss his lips? The thought of his
thighs flanking hers sent a delicious spiral of arousal
through her body. Or, should she sit on his lap and
wrap her arms about his neck?

Beneath the nearly transparent skirts of her French-
inspired gown, her knees wobbled uncontrollably. She
took a baby step forward, sliding one slipper between
the viscount's boots. He moved forward and put his
hands on the backs of her knees, drawing her forward.
She nearly collapsed onto him, but as his hands moved
up the backs of her thighs, she fell onto his lap, so
that when she settled, she found herself cradled in his
embrace. Her arm rested on the top of the camelback

sofa, the pistol dangling from her grip. She sat on the viscount's lap sideways, her legs draped over his. He stared at her, and she lifted her chin, offering her lips.

Lowering his head, he kissed her. And, as his mouth met hers, a streak of exquisite longing washed over Rosalind. The wine-soaked warmth of his breath, the texture of his lips and the wicked deliciousness of his tongue created an unbearably pleasurable sensation. Her body melted as he fitted his mouth to hers, nibbling her lips, kissing her gently, at first.

He drew her more tightly to his chest, and she felt his body stiffen beneath her. His breathing was raspy, his kisses urgent. A throaty moan escaped his throat. There was something terribly erotic, something disturbingly intimate, about staring into his eyes while his arousal intensified. His need excited her; his desire thrilled her. He tore his lips from hers, and kissed her throat. Her head fell back, and she shifted on his lap, wanting nothing more than to press herself as snugly to him as she could, breathing in his scent, feeling the hardness of his body.

"My God, Rosalind. You are beautiful," he whispered, drawing back to look at her. His gaze was warm and tender now, and she felt safe with him. She trusted him. She wanted him.

He dipped his head and planted a kiss on the exposed skin of her décolletage. She felt his hand slide over the swell of bodice, and she gasped. The sensation of his touch was too much for her; in her excitement, every muscle in her body tensed and flexed. Her fingers coiled.

The pistol in her hands exploded and the blast tore through the room like a cannon.

Flung off the viscount's lap, Rosalind landed hard on the floor. Footsteps pounded into the parlor. A babble of male voices erupted above her just as everything faded to blackness.

Three

Rafe jumped to his feet, pivoting to face Tom Wickham and Jemmy Pratt as they burst into the room.

"Are you alright?" Tom asked breathlessly, from the opposite side of the sofa. Rafe's boyhood friend was a stout baby-faced man with curly blond hair.

"God's bones, she's dead!" Jemmy cried.

Rafe hoped that in the confusion, the two men wouldn't find the pistol that had dropped to the floor. He reckoned there was a terrible hole in his carpet as well, but he had no intention of investigating the damage now. Not when this wonderful opportunity to rid himself of Rosalind Yardley had just presented itself.

"Jemmy, go and wake the stable boy. Tell him to bring my carriage around, will you?"

Jemmy hesitated, his jaw slack. "Yardley's chit . . . dead?"

"You advised me to get rid of her," Rafe replied. "Well, she won't talk now."

Tom ran a hand through his riotous curls. "Rafe, this isn't like you."

" 'Spose it had to be done," Jemmy finally said. "I'll go and fetch the carriage."

When Pratt had left the room, Rafe said, "Hand me her cloak over there, would you, Tom?"

His friend moved about the room rather mechanically, as if he were in a daze. When he stood beside Rafe with the cloak in his hands, he said softly, "Did you really have to shoot her, Rafe?"

Rafe snatched the cloak and laid it over Rosalind's motionless body, gently tucking it around her. In a faint, her face was sweet and angelic. He couldn't help but touch her cheek and test the texture of her hair. Then, he straightened, facing Tom.

"She's not dead, Tom. She's merely suffering an attack of the vapors. We were, er . . ."

"Yes, I know. Jemmy and I were coming in from the kitchen, and we got caught on the landing just as you were coming up from the cellar. We thought you wanted your privacy, so we tried to be quiet. Then, Jemmy, well . . . you know Jemmy."

"Perverted character." Rafe ran his hand through his hair. Jemmy was an expert seaman and knew the shoreline and waters between Rye and Brighton better than anyone else. But he possessed a treacherous streak in his character that often concerned Rafe. "I suppose you heard everything, Tom?"

"Not everything. I tugged Jemmy by the sleeve, told him we had no business listening. And then the girl pulled a pistol on you. We couldn't see, but we knew what had happened. I figured we'd better stick around then. In case you needed our help."

"You might have been wise to burst into the parlor

before the gunshot, Tom. She could just as easily have blown a hole in my heart as the Axminster carpet."

"I didn't think she'd ever pull the trigger. I thought you'd easily take the pistol from her, if you wanted to. You're a seasoned smuggler, and she's a green girl. That's one of the reasons I didn't come bursting in before. If you needed me, I was there, Rafe. But, I didn't really expect you'd be put to the test by a young thing like her."

"Thanks for the vote of confidence, dear." The men had been friends for so long, this term of endearment had become a joke. Rafe gave Tom a reassuring pat on the back. "At any rate, we've got an unconscious young woman on our hands. A woman whose father is Sir Sibbald Yardley."

Tom's eyes rounded. "Oh, very good, Rafe. Excellent! What the hell is she doing here?"

Rafe briefly described his encounter with Rosalind in the cavern. "I thought it was Cyril Crawley, and so I lit the lantern. Then, Jemmy came running in, and before I knew it, the girl knew my name, knew of the illegal smuggling operation, and the exact location of our unloading spot."

"Great. Wonderful. Oh, great."

"Anyone ever told you that you've a way with words?" Rafe eyed his friend grimly. Tom had never been the brightest student at Eton, but as a fellow soldier on the Continent, he'd been loyal and brave. The men had risked their necks for each other on more than one occasion. When Annette was ill, Tom devoted himself to helping care for her. And when she died, he hovered over Rafe for nearly six months, well aware of his friend's state of mind, vigilant lest Rafe attempt to end his own life.

"Alright, I'm not as bright as you, and not nearly as handsome. But, you don't see me diddling with magistrate's daughters—"

"I didn't—" Rafe suppressed his laughter. "Diddle her, as you say."

"Well, what are we going to do with her now?"

"We're going to let Jemmy think she's dead, for one thing. I don't want him thinking she's a threat to our operation. 'Twould be a dangerous situation for her."

"What about the danger to us, Rafe? She knows your name, knows where you live. Hell, she knows everything!"

"We have to give her some incentive not to tell her father. Not for a few days, at least. That will give us time to deal with Cyril Crawley, hide our cargo or move in further inland, and pay off our locals so they won't go blabbing when the magistrate's investigators come around."

"Can you trust the locals? One of them is bound to talk, after all."

Rafe lifted his brows, considering. "The magistrate isn't paying for information. We'll pay everybody to keep quiet. Everybody that matters, anyway," he added. "Tomorrow, we'll spend the day in the local taverns and pubs. A little goodwill goes a long way around here." Rafe scratched his chin, thinking. "Besides, the local populace depends heavily on the revenue we bring in from smuggling. They'll protect us, long enough anyway. We only need to divert Sir Sibbald's attention for a month or two. That should be long enough."

"Long enough for what?"

Just then, the crush of gravel beneath carriage wheels sounded at the front of the house. Rafe bent over and gathered the girl in his arms. Her head fell against his shoulder when he stood, and her breath was warm and sweet on his neck. Her weight felt good against his body and as he crossed the floor with her, he had the almost irresistible impulse to continue past the front doors and up the stairs to his bed chamber.

But, Miss Rosalind Yardley was a liability. Miss Rosalind Yardley, with one slip of her tongue, could ruin his livelihood and dispatch him to prison for an eternity. Which was one of the reasons he needed to get rid of her.

The other had to do with his determination never to fall in love again, much less with a woman whom he could never make happy. He had no intention of doing to her what he'd done to Annette, bringing her down to his level, forcing her to live so far away from the city, asking her to give up her family and friends and glittering parties and fancy gowns.

No, he'd made a mistake with Annette. Too late, he'd realized she hadn't happily accepted his life-style, but rather martyred herself to it. It would be the same with Rosalind. She might be infatuated now, but she was bred to marry a duke or an earl, a London aristocrat who would take her to St. James's every season to bow and scrape in front of Prinny's fat figure. She might think he was devilishly exciting, but she wasn't cut out to be a smuggler's bride.

A sleepy-eyed young footman held open the carriage door while Rafe climbed in. Rosalind stirred a bit as he laid her on the leather squabs, but her tiny murmur was unheard by Jemmy, who watched nervously from beneath the portico, or by the driver, who had made the sign of the cross when Rafe emerged from the house with the girl in his arms. As he drew shut the door, Rafe gave Jemmy a sharp salute. To Tom, he threw a rueful smile. Then, he settled on the bench seat opposite Rosalind, and wondered how his life had come to be such a mess.

Slowly, her thoughts coalesced and the darkness that had enveloped her retreated. Rosalind's eyes flickered open and the interior of the carriage, dimly lit by a small lantern beside the door, faded into view. She felt the vibration of wheels beneath her, and an occasional hard jolt. Her head pounded and her eyes felt like they'd been splashed with sand. For a moment, she couldn't remember what had happened.

Then, she turned her head and stared into the smuggler's black gaze. The corners of his lips turned up and his brows lifted speculatively. The confusion, the kiss, and the gunshot came rushing back to her. What a fool she was. She could have killed a man, and why? Because she wanted to show Rafe Lawless that she was not a woman to be trifled with, because she wanted his undivided attention. Because she was attracted to him, and because he'd made her feel like a silly insignificant girl.

The carriage was surprisingly quiet given the obvious speed at which it was eating up the rutted road. Rosalind struggled to her elbows. "Where are you taking me?"

His lean legs were crossed, and he wore an air of elegant, slightly bored, repose. "Back to your daddy."

She sat up, clutching her cloak in her lap. "Back to my father? Are you a Bedlamite? My father will have your neck in a noose before the week is out, *my lord.*"

He looked curious. "Would you have me deliver you elsewhere? Is there a reason you don't want to be returned to your father?"

Bewildered, Rosalind shook her head. Of course, she wanted to go home. On the other hand, the notion of running away and leaving Lady Dovie behind was wildly appealing. She imagined her father wringing his hands and gnashing his teeth, devastated by his beloved daughter's disappearance. He'd be sorry he hadn't paid her more attention, sorry that he'd chosen to marry that frivolous parvenue, that powdered ornament who was an insult to the memory of Rosalind's mother.

"You must take me home, of course," Rosalind said slowly. She closed her eyes, willing herself not to cry.

"You sound as if I am delivering you to Newgate." His voice softened. "Is home such a bad place to be?"

She answered with a too vigorous shake of her head. "My father adores me."

"I'm quite certain of that, Miss Yardley. Indeed, I

suspect you have him wrapped around your little finger."

She smiled at that. She used to. Until Dovie came along.

"Do you have brothers and sisters?"

Looking at the viscount, Rosalind replied, "No, my lord. My mother was never well after I was born. She died when I was ten years old."

"I'm sorry." He uncrossed his legs and leaned forward, staring at her as if he were trying to understand her. "Was it terribly lonely for you growing up?"

The concern in his voice nearly upset her tenuous composure. She wanted him to care, perhaps she even wanted a bit of his sympathy. But, she wanted him to regard her as an adult as well, and his gentle questioning and kind looks were making her feel very vulnerable and childlike.

"How could I be lonely with the scores of governesses and nannies that paraded through our house?" Rosalind tried to force a note of humor into her voice. "And Daddy always had a lady friend to keep him company. He's quite a social animal, Sir Sibbald is. Dinner parties in Brighton during the holidays, hothouse crushes in London during the season."

"Are you lonely *now*?"

She gasped. "If you knew how often I danced at Almack's last spring, you wouldn't ask such a question. 'Struth, my life is crammed with people!"

"A life crammed with people can be terribly lonely."

She let her fake smile slip away. "My dance card was always full last season. I do not want for friends," she said, her voice clipped. "And I have never been lonely."

He ran his hand through his thick black hair, and sighed. "I wonder, though. Three seasons, and not one marriage offer? What the devil is the problem, Miss Yardley? As beautiful as you are, you must have had the young bucks nipping at your heels. I'd wager Sir Sibbald had to beat them off with a stick. But, at the ripe old age of twenty-two, you remain unmarried . . . and if my instincts serve me correctly, a virgin. Do you not like men?"

Heat bloomed in her cheeks, and a wave of panic nearly robbed her of her breath. "How dare you? How dare you ask such an impudent question! 'Tis none of your concern whether I had one marriage proposal or a hundred. Of course I had suitors! Of course I had admirers!"

"But no one that struck your fancy?"

Her jaw worked, but Rosalind couldn't fathom what to say in response. At last, she blurted the truth, or part of it, anyway. "They were all young boys, my lord. Wet behind the ears is what I call it. Tall, gangly things with pimples on their faces and manners as rough as a burlap bag. Not a single one of them had anything to say other than, 'Lovely weather, isn't it, Miss Yardley?' or, 'Do you think the punch is too sweet?' "

"So you're looking for a real man. A grown man. Someone with more sophistication and worldliness."

"Yes. Someone to talk to. Someone who wants to take care of me without smothering me. Someone old enough to appreciate a woman."

"Ah. Someone *exciting.*"

His throaty drawl and half-lidded expression slid over Rosalind's skin like a cashmere blanket. "Yes, I want someone who can excite me." The admission itself, the wickedness of voicing such a thought, sent a jolt of arousal through her veins.

A slow smile spread over his face. The rumble of the carriage wheels was hypnotic, and the flickering light from the lantern accentuated the hard planes and sharp angles of the viscount's face. He pushed off from his bench and sat beside Rosalind, taking her hands in his.

"Are you looking for someone very different from the men you've met before?"

"Perhaps. And you, Lord Pershing? What sort of woman are you looking for?"

He closed his fingers around hers. "To tell the truth, dear girl, I am not looking for any sort of woman. I'm afraid I've given it all up, this business of romance. It's not for me."

"Why not? *Don't you like women?*"

He laughed harshly. "I suppose I deserved that, didn't I? Yes, Miss Yardley, I like women. Very much. But, we can't always have what we want, now can we?"

"You could have any woman you wanted." She held his fingers a bit tighter. "Surely, you must know that."

"You're wrong about that," he replied grimly. "I cannot have the woman I want."

"But you're devilishly handsome, my lord." She noted his self-deprecating smirk. Was it possible he didn't realize how attractive he was? "And you're charming and refined . . . and I believe you kiss very well."

"Thank you, Miss Yardley."

"So, why would a man who could have any woman he wanted choose to be alone?"

" 'Tis better to be alone in some instances than to risk having one's heart broken again. You're too young to understand what I am saying."

"I'm not too young! Someone has hurt you, abandoned you, misused you, even! You say you can't love again because of it! Forgive me, my lord, but I don't believe you. It's just an excuse for not wanting to share your life with anyone else."

His gaze blackened. "If you must know, Miss Yardley, my wife Annette died a few years ago and the simple truth of the matter is that I don't want to love anyone else. There, does that explanation suit you? Not that I owe you any explanation whatsoever. You've caused me quite a bit of trouble tonight, more than you know."

"I'm sorry," Rosalind stammered. "Not about causing you trouble, but about your wife dying. Do you have any children?"

He shook his head, his expression stony.

"Then it is my turn to ask you: are *you* terribly lonely?"

His answering gaze was bleak and defiant.

Thinking she'd pressed him too deeply, she untangled her fingers from his and averted her gaze. Clearly, this was a man who didn't need her comfort and didn't want her friendship. Best to let him grieve for Annette in the private wretchedness of *his* world. She couldn't draw him into her own.

His voice was thick and raspy. "Yes. If you must know, I am lonely."

The hair on the back of her neck prickled. Facing him, she instinctively opened her arms.

He hesitated for no more than an instant. Then, he laid his head on her shoulder and nuzzled the sensitive skin of her neck. His lips were warm, drawing a shiver of guilty pleasure up her spine. "You've held it all inside for much too long, sweetling," he whispered.

Stunned, Rosalind drew in a sharp breath. "You don't know me," she murmured, laying her hand atop his, boldly sliding it along her middle, moving it where she wanted it to go.

He smiled against her neck as his touch roamed the length of her gown. "Perhaps not. But, I know what you want. And what you need."

"Are you arrogant enough to suggest that what I need is you, sir?" Her voice wobbled as she guided his hand over her hips.

"You need a man, Rosalind. And not the sort who will buckle beneath your every whim and temper tantrum. You need a man who will stand toe-to-toe with you, challenge you—"

"Tame me?"

He chuckled. "I suspect you are inordinately spoiled, and accustomed to having your own way."

"Do you think me a shrew?"

He lifted his head and stared at her. "I think you're frightened. But you don't have to be afraid." With her small hand on his, he slowly caressed the soft curve of her belly, the vague outline of her ribs. His fingertips skimmed over the gentle swell of her little bosom, tracing the outline of her low neckline, and teasing gooseflesh to the surface of her bare décolletage.

Rosalind's control rapidly slipped away. She'd never felt anything so pleasurable and it terrified her that in the blink of an eye, she'd become as addicted to him as an opium smoker was to poppy seeds—addicted to his touch, his voice, and to the words he spoke to her.

His hand stilled. He peered into her eyes, waiting. Realizing his silent question, Rosalind's heart thundered. Would she let him go on?

Or would she exercise all the good breeding and religious instruction that had been instilled into her, and tell him to stop?

"Are you going to . . ." She didn't know what, exactly, she was asking.

Grinning, he pressed a finger to her lips. "No Rosalind, I am not going to do anything untoward. But, I am going to kiss you the way no one ever has."

She closed her eyes, utterly fearful yet entirely trusting.

Rafe kissed her lightly first. "And then I am going to return you to your daddy."

The driver's knock on the compartment ceiling signaled their arrival in Brighton. Slowing to a near crawl, the carriage rumbled down the narrow streets of the brightly painted, neatly cobbled, holiday village. Rafe reluctantly lifted his head from the crook of Rosalind's neck. "Sweetling, we're almost there. I'll have to give the driver an address."

Slowly, she pulled her cloak around her shoulders. "From the New Road, head toward North Street. There's a square of houses built round a garden, just off the King's Road. I'll show you when we get there."

Rafe half-stood, opened the ceiling hatch and conveyed the instructions to his driver. Then, he sat beside Rosalind, watching with amusement as she fidgeted beneath his scrutiny.

"Are you alright?" Taking her hand in his, he drew her knuckles to his lips.

A wave of color fanned her cheeks. "Yes, of course. But . . . you won't tell, will you? Father will dispatch me to a nunnery. And he'll discharge Mrs. Childress for neglecting her duties and allowing me to wander off. If he hasn't fired her already, that is. Poor thing, she must be worried sick."

"If she's sobered up. You told me she was a drinker."

"She would have by now." Rosalind bit her lower lip, and stared out the carriage window. Dawn had broken, and the village was awash in cheery pastel tones. But, the mood inside Rafe's carriage had turned quietly somber.

"I'm sorry for what I've done," Rosalind said, blinking back tears.

Rafe took a deep breath, squeezed Rosalind's fingers, then released them. Rosalind's regret surprised him. Last night, she had seemed determined not only to make mischief, but to taste independence.

"I'm sorry, too, then." Wishing to put some distance between himself and her, he moved to the opposite bench. "Don't worry, no one need ever know."

She shut her eyes. "What will I tell Father? He'll ask me where I've been, you know. Young women don't go wandering off without their nannies. It's unheard of! He'll interrogate me as if I were the very worst sort of criminal. He'll suspect something terrible, of course. I'll have to tell him something."

"I've been thinking about that." Rafe folded his arms across his chest. What he had to say pained him. He didn't like deceiving Rosalind, especially after the intimacies they'd shared. He rather liked the woman—when she wasn't playing the role of spoiled daddy's girl, that is. "You cannot tell him the truth, Rosalind."

"No, he'd have you hanged." She looked at him, wide-eyed.

"I'm afraid that's not all." He forced himself to meet her pale-blue gaze. "You'd have a heap of trouble yourself. And not just because you allowed me to kiss you in my carriage on the trip from Hastings to Brighton."

"I wouldn't tell that part, sir."

"Nor would I. A gentleman never would. But, I would tell of something else that had happened during your short stay at my seaside home. Do you recall shooting someone, Rosalind?"

Her lips slowly parted. She said nothing, but stared at him in disbelief.

Hating himself, Rafe continued. He had to, not just to protect himself, but to protect the lives and livelihoods of his men. Even Cyril Crawley's career was at stake, and the fat man had somehow sired eight children. They'd all go hungry if Rosalind Yardley blabbed to her daddy about what she'd seen on the beach below the cliff where the bonfires were burning. "Don't you remember pulling the trigger?"

She shook her head.

"You do remember the pistol, don't you?"

"I remember slipping it out of the waistband of your breeches," she whispered. "I hid it in the folds of my cloak. Then, I took it out in the parlor and waved it at you. But, I didn't mean to—"

"No, I'm sure you didn't. But, then we were on the sofa and things were, well, they were rather havey-cavey, weren't they?"

"It all happened so quickly."

"Precisely. But, what happened, dear girl, is that you accidentally discharged the pistol. It's hardly surprising. You were nervous and afraid. You'd been knocked off balance and you didn't realize what you were doing."

"I shot someone." Her face had turned pale and her lips bloodless.

A streak of guilt shot through Rafe's body, but he gritted his teeth and plunged on. He owed nothing to this girl, he told himself. She was spoiled and flighty and too insincere even to admit that she'd taken pleasure from his kisses. He hated to admit it, but perhaps she was getting her comeuppance. Perhaps she'd learn a lesson or two from this experience. God knows, she could benefit from a dose of growing-up powder.

"You shot one of my men. He was hiding beneath a refectory table on the other side of the room. Turns out he was in the parlor when we came up the stairs. Looking for snuff as best I can tell. There was tobacco all over him, and the box I keep in my desk was empty."

"He must have heard us coming."

"He didn't want to be caught pilfering my snuff, so he hid beneath the table."

"The room was dark, we didn't see him."

"He hoped to sneak out. When we were on the sofa—" Rafe leaned forward, his elbows propped on his knees.

"—I pulled the trigger. By accident." Rosalind covered her face with her hands, and moaned. After a few minutes, she peeked through her fingers, and whispered, "Did I kill him?"

Rafe hesitated. If he told the girl she'd killed someone, she'd as like have a nervous collapse. Or worse. In the end, he simply couldn't burden her with that monumental a source of guilt. "No . . . but he won't father any more children, I'm afraid."

"Oh." Her hands fell to her lap, and she looked at him with an expression of pure agony. "I shot a man in the—"

"Never seen so much blood," Rafe murmured absently.

Her voice was barely audible. "I'm ever so sorry."

"I understand." Rafe stroked his chin. "Of course, the question now is, what to do?"

"Who was the man?" Her tears inexplicably vanished. Drying her face with the back of her hand, she pinned Rafe with a determined gaze. "What is the man's name? Tell me, I must know."

"His name? You needn't bother yourself with that, Rosalind. I'll handle all the arrangements, see that he receives proper medical care, that sort of thing. I take care of my men, you see. It's part of my job."

"I see." Frowning, she twisted her fingers. "But, I need to know his name. I must try and make it up to him somehow."

Seeing his opportunity, Rafe gently touched Rosalind's knee. "I'll tell you how you can make it up to him. And save your own hide into the bargain. Tell your father that you got lost wandering on the beach, that you stumbled over some rocks and fainted. You didn't hear his search party, you didn't know how many hours had passed. They must have passed right by you! But, it was a dark, starless night, and unless someone shined a *touchier* directly over you, you'd have been invisible."

"You're asking me to lie to my father."

"I'm asking you to save a man's life. If you tell your father everything you've seen, he'll have me arrested before sunset. All my men, too, except things will go much worse for them. Without title or wealth or political influence, they'll end up in a musty, rat-infested gaol. Or on a prison ship bound for Australia. Either way, the man you shot won't survive his punishment. Surely, you understand."

A film of tears glittered in her eyes, but she dashed them away with the edge of her cloak. "Of course."

"And in return, I won't tell anyone that you shot, er, Mr. Fellowes."

"Fellowes? Is that his name?"

"Redd Fellowes to be exact. Feisty sort, with a wife who's always pregnant and a ma who can't stay out of the bottle. If he couldn't earn a living, why they'd all starve."

"Will he ever be able to . . ."

"Walk again? Yes, I think so. I'll find some work for him to do. Get him on the next ship going to a warm clime, if I can." Rafe gave her a crooked grin. "His poor little wife might actually be grateful to know there won't be any more babes on the way . . . not after the one she's carrying is delivered that is."

Two little pinches of color appeared in Rosalind's cheeks. Glancing out the carriage window, she spotted the familiar houses of her street and pointed out her own. Rafe tapped the ceiling, and the carriage ground to a halt.

"There isn't much time." It made him nervous to be parked right in front of Sir Sibbald Yardley's town house. He wanted to be gone from there as quickly as possible. "Do we have an understanding, then?"

She smiled demurely. "Yes. Whatever happened tonight will never be spoken of again."

He reached for her and squeezed her fingers. "Never."

She paused, her lashes flickering nervously. "Last night . . . all I've done . . . 'twas most out of character for me . . ."

He leaned forward and laid his fingertip on her lips. "I'll always cherish the memory, sweetling. I'll never tell a soul."

Her gaze met his. "No, I don't suppose you would."

Regret and guilt tugged at Rafe's heart. He thought for an instant that chivalry required him to pull her back into his arms, then drive like a demon toward Gretna Green and marry Miss Rosalind Yardley. And he might have done so, but the memory of Annette's disapprobation and discontent was fresh in his mind.

"If I ever meet you again, Rosalind, we will be as strangers. Do you understand?"

"Yes." She had regained her composure now. She pressed her lips together, determined and strong. The spoiled daddy's girl he'd encountered last night had a backbone of steel this morning. "Yes . . . and Lord Pershing? One last thing."

"What is it?"

"Thank you."

He grazed her knuckles with his lips. "Never kiss a man who doesn't love you, sweetling. Promise me that."

"I promise," she whispered as the carriage door opened.

"I don't think we should stay in this neighborhood much longer," Rafe's young footman said, offering his hand to Rosalind.

Handing her out of the carriage, Rafe despised himself. Deceiving Rosalind, tricking her into remaining silent about his smuggling enterprise, was the very worst sort of chicanery he'd ever perpetrated on a woman. But, then, he was accustomed to feeling like a fraud. He'd felt like one ever since he realized

Annette's unhappiness, ever since he realized she didn't really like him.

She turned and smiled at him before the footman slammed shut the carriage door. Through the window, he watched her pull her cloak around her and head dutifully for the glossy black lacquered front door of her father's house. The carriage took off with a lurch and Rafe was jolted back on the leather bench seat. His head ached from lack of sleep. His chest ached from guilt. And his body ached with desire for one Miss Rosalind Yardley.

Four

The front door was unlocked, and she made it up the stairs without encountering a single servant. She found Sir Sibbald and Lady Dovie in the breakfast room, seated at the dining table, looking tired and confused.

"Good morning, Father. Hello, Dovie."

They looked up, their eyes round. For a moment, the room was silent. A servant entered from the kitchen door, saw Rosalind standing on the threshold, and nearly dropped the platter of sausages she was taking to the sideboard.

Suddenly, Sir Sibbald and Dovie sprang into action. They bolted from the table and rushed to Rosalind, their arms open wide.

"Oh, thank God! You've come home safely!" Sir Sibbald drew his daughter into his arms, nearly smothering her in his snuff-scented embrace.

With her head on her father's broad shoulder, her tiptoes suspended off the floor, Rosalind squeaked, "Hello, Father. I can't breathe."

"Oh, my." Releasing her, he held her at arm's

length, peering into her eyes, then scanning her figure from head to toe. "Are you quite alright? You must tell me, child, where have you been?"

"We've nearly worried ourselves to death," chimed in Lady Dovie. She gave Rosalind a quick peck on the cheek, then laid a restraining hand on her husband's arm. "Sit down, the two of you. Rosalind, you must be starved. Mrs. Hennipen, bring a plate, will you? And some strong tea for Miss Rosalind."

Rosalind sat at her father's right hand, across from Lady Dovie. Mrs. Hennipen quickly laid a heavily laden plate in front of her, and the aroma of sausages and eggs and yeasty rolls with caramel toppings caused her mouth to water. Rosalind ate heartily, and as if she'd never been taught how to use a knife and fork. Tucking into her food seemed a reasonable response to having been missing overnight, and it gave her an excuse to evade many of the incisive questions her father set about asking her.

"Where have you been, child?" Sir Sibbald was a tall, imposing man with thinning gray hair and a hawkish nose. To some, he appeared imperious and intimidating. Rosalind perceived him as a man lacking any character flaw, a trait, which, she had derived, made him unobtainable to her. Unless she married royalty, she could never hope to impress him with her achievements.

She had his attention now, though. "On the beach, most of the evening."

"On the beach?" Dovie's eyes popped.

"Were you lost?"

Rosalind chewed a bite of sausage, considering her

answer. "For a while, I suppose. I got bored with the bonfires, and decided to go for a walk."

"On the beach?" asked Dovie.

"Alone?" Sir Sibbald queried.

"Yes. Well, I couldn't bear it anymore. There was no one at the party I cared to talk to. They were all your friends, not mine."

"But how did you slip away from Mrs. Childress?" Now this was going to be a tricky area to circumnavigate. Rosalind was loath to tell her father, the crusader against smuggling, that Mrs. Childress spent most of her earnings on contraband brandy. The old woman had been Rosalind's nursemaid, nanny and companion since she was a toddler. After her mother's death, Rosalind relied heavily on Mrs. Childress's comforting presence, despite the woman's obvious drinking problem. Now that she was in her dotage, she'd have no other place to go if Sir Sibbald turned her out.

So, for the past few years, Rosalind had been assisting her chaperone in covering up her nearly constant state of intoxication. It put a strain on Rosalind, to say the least, but tattling on Mrs. Childress was not an option.

"Mrs. Childress was cold, so I told her to go back to the carriage."

"The poor woman is so distraught," Dovie interjected. "We haven't been able to make sense of a word she's said."

"She's taken to her bed." Sir Sibbald shook his head, but his stern gaze never left Rosalind's face. "Babbling like the village idiot and refusing to take any food. My God, we thought we were going to have to commit her. Would have, I suppose, if you hadn't shown up."

Rosalind gestured for the dour-faced Mrs. Hennipen standing guard by the kitchen door. "Would you send word to Mrs. Childress, please, that I have returned home and that I'm alright. Tell her I'm sorry that I gave her the slip. And I'll be up soon to see about her."

When the servant had left the room, Sir Sibbald cocked his head, squinted his eyes, and studied his daughter as if through a telescope. "Hungry, are you?"

"Starving," Rosalind said around a buttered roll.

"But, you seem none the worse for wear. Where did you sleep, if I may ask?"

His somewhat challenging tone sent a sliver of dread through Rosalind's heart. Her father was a master interrogator, trained to discern whether his informants were telling the truth or simply leading him on a wild-goose chase. She wasn't up to tricking him, she couldn't possibly hope to. And yet she had to. Otherwise her life, and the lives of Mr. Fellowe's starving brats, would be ruined.

"I don't know, Daddy. I fell down, you see. On the beach. Near the cliff. I must have tripped over some flotsam, or slipped on a wet rock."

"The headlands are treacherous," Dovie agreed.

"At any rate, I remember turning my ankle, and a streak of pain shot through me. I don't recall what happened after that, but I must have fainted. When I awoke, I was dreadfully cold and the sun was coming up. My ankle hurt, but I managed to make it back to the path that led from the cliff to the beach. A passing carriage stopped and delivered me here."

"Who was it?" her father demanded. "I should like to thank him, or her."

Rosalind shook her head. "It was some lord's driver. The carriage was empty. I didn't think to ask who it belonged to."

"Rosalind! What manners!" Dovie looked askance.

"Manners? What do I care about her blasted manners at a time like this?" Sir Sibbald's face was dark with emotion and the vein at his temple throbbed. "My daughter spent the night on the beach, injured. She could have died from exposure, or been attacked by a band of brigands or pirates."

"Oh, Daddy, there aren't any pirates anymore." Rosalind drained her cup of tea and set it down with a clatter. "Really, I am quite alright. And after a hot bath and a good nap, I'm sure I'll be even better."

She felt her stepmother's skeptical stare and she looked the woman in the eye. "Something on your mind, Lady Dovie?"

The woman cut her eyes at Sir Sibbald and frowned. "No, nothing, it's just that . . . no, nothing."

"I'm going to send Mrs. Hennipen to fetch the surgeon," Sir Sibbald said. "She'll need her ankle tended to."

"No, Daddy, really—"

"I insist, Rosalind. You've had a bad scare. We all have. And I, for one, am not certain you're telling the truth."

Rosalind's heart hammered. "Not telling the truth?"

"Mrs. Childress is abovestairs acting as though she's had the shock of her life. No doubt due to the guilt she feels at having let you out of her sight. Good God, I should have fired her on the spot last night, the moment I learned you were missing!"

"Daddy, please don't!" Rosalind went to her father, bent down and put her arms around his neck. "It wasn't Nanny's fault, really. She was watching the bonfires, and I told her I was going to meet Lady Toppainsley. She had no reason to think I would change my mind, and take a walk on the beach."

"But, it was so cold last night," Lady Dovie murmured. "And windy."

"I told you, I was bored." Rosalind, who was much too big and too old to sit on her father's lap, did so, anyway. "Daddy, don't be angry with Mrs. Childress."

But, instead of wrapping her in his warm embrace, Sir Sibbald pushed her off his lap and held her at arm's length. "I wonder, child. Why isn't your gown drenching wet? If you stumbled and spent the night on the beach . . ."

"Look, my slippers are ruined!" Rosalind lifted the hem of her skirts and showed him the water stains on her satin slippers.

"Even a raw young brute of a man would find sleeping on the beach a trying experience. How is it that a delicate little girl—"

"Daddy, I'm not a delicate little girl!" Rosalind propped her fists on her hips, genuinely angered by her father's condescension. "And I'll brook no more of this. Either you believe me, or you don't. What would you have me say, that I was kidnapped by a gang of smugglers? Would that satisfy your lust for vengeance, Daddy?"

He rose to his full height and towered over Rosalind. "I'll not have my daughter speak to me in such an insolent tone. You gave your nanny the slip, Rosalind, and spent the night unchaperoned on a stretch of dangerous beach. Your stepmother and I nearly worried ourselves crazy speculating on what tragedy had befallen you. Then, you show up this morning, looking for all the world as if you've had some great adventure with your pink cheeks and disheveled hair, and you expect me to believe that you stumbled over a rock, passed out, and spent the night on the beach."

"A stranger gave me a ride into town." Rosalind picked a spot at the bridge of her father's nose and made herself stare at it. "By the time I arrived here, my clothes were dry. I'm sorry you worried about me, Father, but, quite frankly, I resent your skepticism. I fell over a rock and fainted, and that is all there is to it."

For a moment, Rosalind and her father stood toe to toe, their gazes locked in a contest of wills. Lady Dovie sat frozen, her lips parted, her eyes wide. In distant regions of the house, servants could be heard bustling about, rattling pots and pans, treading the carpeted stairs, chattering with one another as they cleaned, polished, dusted, and gathered laundry. It seemed to Rosalind, however, that her world had spun to a dead stop. Her future hung in the balance;

if her father refused to believe her rather flimsy fabrication, she'd have a devil of a time concealing the awful truth from him.

At length, her father's expression softened. He continued to stare at her through one eye, as if he couldn't quite focus clearly enough on her, but his jaw lost its stony edge and his prominent chin descended a notch. "Alright then, Rosalind. If that's the way you want it, then I shall go along with your little story.

"It isn't a *little story,*" Rosalind replied quietly.

Her father merely lifted his brows, jerked his head toward the door, and said, "Get a hot bath and then get into bed. You'll be lucky if you don't catch your death of cold, young lady."

"Thank you, Father." But Sir Sibbald was already seated at the table, his back to her.

For once, Rosalind was glad to see his interest in her fade. With a sigh of relief, she turned and rushed from the room. At the threshold, she drew to a halt, reined in abruptly by her father's booming voice.

Without looking at her, he said, "I'm glad to see, Rosalind, that the ankle you injured last night has miraculously healed itself."

"Thank you, Father," she whispered, as she continued, half-limping this time, out the door.

"We're in a heap of trouble, Nanny."

The older woman's hair was a nimbus of frazzled steel. Propped against a bank of pillows, she looked more tired than weak, as if she'd suffered more from a long night of drinking than from the shock of losing her charge. But her eyes twinkled with happiness at Rosalind's appearance.

At Rosalind's suggestion of trouble, the aging nursemaid frowned. "What sort of trouble, Rosie?"

"I haven't quite told all the truth." Rosalind, seated on the edge of the bed, leaned forward. "The story I told Father is only part of what happened. But, you must know the truth, so that you can help me."

Mrs. Childress made the sign of the cross. "Sweet Jesus. What sort of bumblebroth have you gotten yourself into now, girl?"

"I didn't fall on the beach. Well, I did fall, but I didn't faint." Rosalind closed her eyes, harkening back to what had indeed transpired. "Actually, I did faint—"

"Lord, girl! Just tell me what happened!"

Rosalind took a deep breath, and in a tumble of words, spilled the entire sordid story. The only part that she omitted was what happened inside the carriage on the journey between Rye and Brighton. Even the thought of Lord Pershing's kisses was enough to incite a warm flush. But she couldn't dwell on that now. At the moment, she had to enlist her faithful companion's complicity and silence.

"That's why I have to get back to Rye," she concluded, squeezing Mrs. Childress's hand.

"No, Rosalind, that is precisely why you must stay away from there! And pour me some more tea while you are about, will you?"

Rosalind reached for the pot on the bedside table.

She refilled an empty cup, and placed it in Mrs. Childress's trembling hands.

"There's a little medicine beneath my pillow," Mrs. Childress said. "Would you mind?"

Rosalind slipped her fingers beneath the mound of pillows and found a tiny brown stoppered bottle. Yanking the cork, she gave her old nanny a frown. "Father would have us both tossed in the street if he knew about this, Mrs. C."

"Purely for medicinal purposes, Rosie." The older woman tapped Rosalind's hand, causing a rather judicious amount of brandy to pour into her tea. "It relieves the ache in my old bones, and softens the blow to my senses when I hear you rattle on about such ridiculous affairs as getting kidnapped by a smuggler, then shooting an invisible accomplice. And now you tell me you want to go back there, and get yourself in even deeper trouble."

"But don't you see, I must! If I shot a man, then I must make amends. I have some money saved, Mrs. C., a small account left me by my mother. When I find this Mr. Fellowes, I'll arrange to have the money transferred to him and his family. If his children need clothing, I can send them my old cast-offs. If they need food—"

"Why not just ask them to live here?" Mrs. Childress stared at Rosalind over the rim of her teacup. "Perhaps Sir Sibbald will take them all in, adopt the entire lot of them, treat them as family."

"Don't ridicule me, please." Sensing that Mrs. Childress was not coming about as easily as she'd have predicted, Rosalind leaned forward. "I've done plenty for you, haven't I? And we've always stuck together, haven't we? The two musketeers, isn't that what we used to call ourselves?"

Mrs. Childress sighed. "You aren't going to blackmail me, are you? I am well aware that you've kept your lips sealed about the delivery boy who comes round here, but I won't be blackmailed, dear. Tell your father if you want. I can find another place of employment any time I want to."

"What sort of girl do you think I am? I would *never* dream of telling Daddy about your cache of brandy. My goodness, think how embarrassing that would be to him. Given Daddy's position, I mean. Imagine the newspaper headlines: *Anti-smuggling crusader finds contraband whisky in his own home*. Why, he'd faint from the humiliation alone!"

"You *are* blackmailing me, aren't you?"

Rosalind gave her friend a smile as sweet as treacle. "No, dear, I am merely agreeing that there are some things Daddy needn't know."

"One of them being the fact you shot a man, and now you want to make amends by giving him your scuffed up slippers."

"You make me sound so . . . so shallow!"

Mrs. Childress stared at her a long time without speaking. At length, she responded in a quiet, weary voice. "I don't think you are shallow, Rosie. If I've had any influence on you at all, I hope it has been to instill a kindness in your heart, a willingness to try to understand the troubles of people from all walks of life. If I thought you were like one of those bleeding-heart, political reformist suffragettes who chatter on and on about the importance of helping the *poor people* while never once lifting a finger to actually help one of them, I would be very disappointed in you."

"Just so," Rosalind murmured, attempting to absorb Mrs. Childress's warning. Was she, in fact, as vapid and self-absorbed as one of those ladies her nanny had described? Was her motivation for wanting to find Redd Fellowes purely a selfish one?

Her nanny's words resonated. Rosalind's shoulders slumped a bit as she considered the foolhardiness of her previous twelve hours. Giving Mrs. C. the slip was an act of rebellion, the defiant prank of a repressed schoolgirl. Kissing a stranger in a deserted cave was pure folly, dangerous caprice, for which she paid the heavy price of being kidnapped. Kissing him again once he had her in his captivity was even sillier. What had she hoped to gain from that escapade, other than a few minutes of guilty pleasure?

And, the carriage trip home . . . her cheeks stung at the thought of the moments she'd shared with Rafe Lawless, Viscount Pershing. Burying her face in her hands, Rosalind stifled a sob. She was tired and sleep-deprived. She had broken every rule her father had ever laid down for her. She'd violated his trust, and, if he ever learned the truth of what she'd done with Viscount Pershing, he'd send her to Egypt on holiday with a one-way ticket and a hardy goodbye. She'd shot a man, and her motivation for making amends was ill-conceived and selfish. What sort of person was she, indeed? It was a question she hadn't asked herself nearly often enough, and one that she was finding difficult to answer now.

"Sometimes we must look at ourselves in a critical way," Mrs. Childress said softly, as if she could read Rosalind's mind. "But, why don't you get some sleep now, and we will talk about it when you are rested? Thing may seem clearer, then."

"I'm so tired." Standing, Rosalind wiped her tear-stained face with the back of her hand. She bent down and gave Mrs. Childress a peck, inhaling the familiar aroma of brandy and mint that had surrounded her nanny the past few years, since the woman had fallen and hurt her hip so badly and the doctors hadn't been able to eradicate her pain. "Thank you, Mrs. C."

"I'm afraid I haven't made you feel any better, Rosie."

"You didn't ease my conscience, that's true." Rosalind forced a wobbly smile to her lips. "I suppose I've plenty to think about, though, thanks to you. Only a true friend would dare tell me what you have, Mrs. C."

"You're a good girl, Rosie. I've always believed in you."

Another sob threatened to shatter Rosalind's composure. Consumed by guilt and remorse for what she'd done in the past twelve hours, she bit her lip and tamped down her emotion. It wouldn't do to break down in front of Mrs. Childress. It would only upset the woman, and she was already feeling poorly.

"I'm so sorry—" Rosalind gulped in a deep breath.

"Oh, my. Don't say it. You've no need—"

"Yes, yes, I must! I'm sorry for leaving you at the bonfire. You must have been dreadfully worried about me! And to think you had to face Daddy's anger alone . . . while I was in Rye, having a . . . an adventure! Oh, Mrs. Childress, I promise I'll never behave that irresponsibly again!"

The older woman looked shrewd. "I don't believe you will, dear."

"I've learned my lesson."

"You've learned *one.*"

"I'll never let myself be swept away by a man again!"

Her nanny chuckled. "Like I said, dear, you've learned one lesson. But, you have many more to learn before you're done on this earth. We all have."

Sniffing, Rosalind squared her shoulders. "So do you think I should abandon my plan to find this man, Redd Fellowes? Isn't it worse to ignore the fact I injured him?"

"Far worse. No, dear, I think you should find him, and do whatever you can to make amends. I merely want you to understand your underlying emotions about what has happened. You've shot a man, or so you say . . . *or so that bounder Lord Pershing says.* And now you want to track him down and see for yourself what damage you've done. You want to offer him a token of your remorse. You want to feel better about yourself, and about the wrong you've committed."

Rosalind lifted her chin a notch. "Is that so very wrong?"

Mrs. Childress didn't answer. But, she did peer up at Rosalind with an expression of mixed amusement and censure. "You're not telling the whole story, are you, Rosie?"

"You're a sly old tabby, Mrs. C." Rosalind drew in a deep breath and planted her fists on her hips. "Are you going to help me, or not?"

"Yes, dear, I am going to help you. Was there ever any doubt?"

No, Rosalind thought. But the relief she felt was minimal compared to the fear clutching at her heart. Practically overnight, her world had turned topsy-turvy. She'd defied her father, then lied to him. She'd brazenly kissed one man, then accidentally shot another. And, to make matters more complicated than she'd ever thought possible, she'd allowed a dangerous criminal—a man she couldn't afford to like, much less love—to touch her heart in a way no other man ever had.

Rafe Lawless, Viscount Pershing, sat with two other men at a scarred wooden table in the back corner of The Salty Dog, a half-timbered tavern on the outskirts of Rye. The row of bottles in the greasy window had reputedly been there since Shakespeare's day, and the dank atmosphere reeked of medieval debauchery. But the owner was one of Rafe's most loyal customers, and the place was a safe haven where men could congregate to drink beer or brandy in relative anonymity.

Jemmy Pratt, his snout full of beer, slammed his bottle on the table. "So ye took me advice, did ye? Got rid of the gel, did ye?"

Rafe felt Tom Wickham's keen gaze, but kept his

own trained on Jemmy. "You needn't worry about her tattling to the authorities."

" 'Twas her father I was worried about!" Jemmy lifted his hand and summoned another beer. When the proprietor had plunked down another round of tankards, he took another long draft, half-draining it. With the back of his hand, he wiped a moustache of foam from his lips. Then, elbows on the table, he leaned forward, staring his challenge at Rafe. "One little word from that fancy tart, and we'd all be hanging from a scaffold."

"She's not—" Hot blood boiled up in Rafe's veins. "She *was* not a *fancy tart.*"

The viscount's imperious tone and his glacier-like glare momentarily rebuffed Jemmy Pratt. The young seafarer sat back in his chair and looked quizzically at Tom Wickham. At length, he turned his scrutiny back to Rafe. "Do I detect a note of *admiration* in your voice, mate? You didn't go soft over that little fish, did ye?"

"I told you I got rid of her, Pratt. That's all you need to know."

"Look, Pratt," Tom interjected. "Don't rock the boat. Let sleeping dogs lie."

"One thing I can say for you, Tom, dear, is that you're never trite." Rafe laughed grimly while Tom's cheeks darkened with embarrassment.

Jemmy, however, wasn't amused. "I ain't gonna let go of this, *my lord*. What did you do to the girl?"

"You saw me get in the coach with her lifeless body, didn't you?"

"I ain't sure what I seen."

Rafe's patience evaporated. "Then be sure of this, Pratt. The girl's no threat to us now. I fixed all that. Now, don't ask any more questions, because the less you know about it, the better off you are."

"There's somethin' about it I don't like." Pratt drained his tankard and pushed to his feet. Standing, he wobbled a bit, and, fortified by beer, brazenly pointed a finger at the viscount. "Something about this smells as rank as a two-week-old haddock."

Tom sprang to his feet and held up his hands, nervously patting the air. "That's the beer talking, Pratt. You're going to be sorry that you provoked Lord Pershing when you've sobered up."

The drunken sailor snarled an obscenity, gave Rafe a mocking salute, then turned on his heel. As he made for the door, Pratt listed to the starboard side as if he were walking the deck of a ship about to keel over. When he was gone, Tom resumed his seat while Rafe took a healthy gulp of beer and willed his muscles to relax.

"Don't worry, Rafe. The man's a Bedlamite."

"He might be. But he's a mite too interested in Miss Yardley for my comfort."

With his fingertips, Tom traced an invisible pattern on the scarred tabletop. At length, he screwed up the courage to ask, "So, what exactly did happen between you and the girl?"

Rafe stared so hard that his friend actually flinched. "What the devil are getting at? Do you think I've gone soft over the chit, too? Do you think I'd compromise my enterprise and the safety of all the men who work for me just because I took a fancy to a pretty little green girl?"

"She was terribly young."

"She's twenty-two."

Tom lifted his brows. "Really? And never been married? Well, what's the matter with her?"

A thread of irritation knotted in Rafe's heart. In the short time he'd known Rosalind, he'd felt compelled to come to her defense more than once, in more ways than one. It made her somewhat of a bother; on the other hand, the notion that he could furnish her some protection was strangely appealing.

"Why assume there's anything the matter with her, Tom? More likely she hasn't yet met a man who's worthy of her."

"Ah." Tom nodded knowingly, but there was a glint of amusement in his eyes. "And how was the carriage ride back to Brighton? Any interesting developments?"

"What the hell do you mean by that?"

"I mean, what did you say to her? What sort of conversation did you have? How can you be so certain she won't tell her father what she saw on the beach?"

"Because she won't, that's why." After a moment, during which Tom stared disbelievingly at him, Rafe added, "I've convinced her it's in her best interest to keep her pretty lips sealed. She fainted when the gun went off in her hands, you know. I told her she shot someone."

"Shot someone? Did she really buy that story?"

"Hook, line, and sinker. She's scared to death. If she blabs, her involvement in a crime will be exposed.

Believe me, she's got plenty of incentive to keep quiet."

"Yes, I suppose you're right. And I'm glad you didn't have to hurt her. She seemed like an interesting young woman, if not a bit immature."

"Immature?" The criticism rankled. Rafe leaned back in his chair and pictured Rosalind Yardley daring him to kiss her, then waving a pistol about with a recklessness that was frightening. Perhaps she was a bit . . . unschooled. Annette had been equally fearless, and though sheltered by her doting parents, exceedingly rebellious in her own way.

"I didn't mean—" Tom started.

"No need to apologize. You're right. These wealthy Brighton girls are exotic little creatures. Coddled by their nannies and ignored by their parents, they come out of the schoolroom with manners as constricting as Prinny's corset. They might seem immature, but in truth, they're just naive. Most of them do their duty and get married, and have babies, ignoring their husbands' infidelities and living happily ever after. Apparently."

"And those who don't?"

Rafe pinched the bridge of his nose, remembering Annette, remembering her defiance as they raced toward Gretna Green, toward her freedom and the life she claimed to want above all else. "The others? Well, they chafe against their parents' restrictions until they escape . . ."

Or until they die, Rafe thought.

Tom swallowed a mouthful of beer. "And which category does Miss Rosalind Yardley fit into?"

Rafe smiled crookedly at his friend. "I'm afraid I would need something far stronger than beer to continue this conversation. Suffice to say that Rosalind Yardley is older than she looks, and more mature than she gives off. She's eager to escape her parents' restrictions, all right, but she hasn't quite learned what she wants to do after that."

Tom slapped his companion on the back. "Well, let's hope she doesn't pull free from her moorings before she's set a course for her destination."

Rafe laughed, his anxiety fading.

"Shall we shift the subject, now?"

"Happily."

"We've been invited to a party, my lord. A very exclusive party at Lord and Lady Toppainsley's town home in Brighton."

"Those pretentious nabobs? Why in the world would they invite parvenus like us to a party?"

Tom smiled. "Why wouldn't they? There's nothing unsavory about us, Rafe. Why, for all Lord Toppainsley knows, we're as sober as two judges and as virginal as nuns. He's a right sporting fellow, if you ask me. I met him this morning at the Spanish Coin tavern in Brighton—"

"This morning? When you were making a delivery?" A bubble of suspicion rose in Rafe's throat.

Tom threaded his fingers through his unruly curls. "Actually, I was playing a hand of cards and having a morning eye-opener. Toppainsley came in, dressed like Beau Brummel in the handsomest suit I've ever seen. Boots so shiny a man could see his reflection in them."

"He's a bit of a dandy," Rafe murmured.

"Yes, but he's a regular buck. Down to earth and all that. Tells a hell of a joke about the Prince and Mrs. Fitzherbert, but it wouldn't do to repeat it in mixed company—"

"Yes, yes, and then he simply asked you to his party, just like that?"

Tom shrugged. "Pretty much. We'd played a few hands of cards, shared some conversation. He agrees with us about these taxes on imported wine. Thinks they're disgraceful, thinks the lords who voted on 'em ought to be—"

"You didn't tell him—"

"Tell him what, Rafe? That I'm engaged in a smuggling enterprise at the present moment? That the contraband brandy he was drinking came across the channel just hours ago, with my best friend Viscount Pershing at the helm, and me below deck counting oak barrels of Bordeaux? Bloody ballocks, Rafe . . . do you think I'm an idiot?"

With a sigh, Rafe shook his head. "Of course not."

Tom sulked for no more than an instant, then took a drink of beer and brightened. "Look, old man, I thought it would do us good. When Toppainsley invited me to his party, I wrangled an invitation for you, too. *'The more the merrier,'* the dandy cried. And, so, we're invited. I think we should go. Who knows? We might meet some interesting women, there, Rafe. I don't know about you, but I've had quite a dry spell, lately."

The image of Rosalind, her lips slightly parted in surprise, her cheeks flushed, flashed in Rafe's mind.

His interlude with her the night before had left him edgy, irritable, and hungry for a female. He couldn't quite characterize his recent love life as a dry spell— Rafe had never lacked for willing women in his entire adult, unmarried life.

But, Miss Rosalind Yardley had tweaked some deeply buried emotions, feelings he would have just as soon kept hidden inside. And the best medicine he could think of to counter those emotions was a little good old-fashioned wenching.

Yes, he'd go to Toppainsley's party, and, perhaps he would find a willing woman interested in some uncomplicated bed play.

He might also satisfy his curiosity about Lord Toppainsley. And if the man was as rabidly anti-government as Tom Wickham believed he was, he might acquire a new customer as well.

Five

"Step on my heels once more, Mrs. Childress, and you will rip the hem off this ridiculously expensive ball gown!"

"Pardon me, child." The older woman slipped an oriental paper fan from her reticule and fanned herself. "I didn't expect such a hothouse crush in Brighton. La, I wouldn't have thought there were so many desirable people in this little village."

"Half of Mayfair is here this time of year," replied Rosalind. "There's nothing going on in London, and since Prinny has turned this resort town into his own romantic hideaway, everybody who is anybody wants to be seen here."

Mrs. Childress's eyes popped wide as she scanned the room. "I've never seen such flimsy dresses. Look at that lady across the room, Rosie. When the light behind her shines just so, I can see the outline of her—"

Rosalind glanced at the pretty young woman whose cream colored gown was as substantial as a whisper. Indeed, the silhouette of her hips was visible when she stood at a certain angle. "She mustn't be very modest. Or else she doesn't know—"

Mrs. Childress gave her gentle nudge. "She knows. There, see if you can get around these horrid people and let's find the punch table, shall we?"

A manservant in bright blue breeches materialized with a tray on which two cups of frothy punch were perched. Rotating the tray, he offered a cup to Rosalind. Sighing with relief, Mrs. Childress took the other cup from the tray. "Past the teeth and over the gums . . ." Then, the older woman raised her drink to Rosalind's and gave a saucy wink of approval.

Wending her way through the crowd, Rosalind noticed several women dressed in unusually daring gowns, either too low-cut to be acceptable in Mayfair drawing rooms, or too gauzy to be considered decent. They seemed to float through the ballroom, casting sly smiles at the men, ignoring the sidelong glaces of the other ladies. The realization that there were demi-reps and courtesans at the party rippled through Rosalind like a wicked thrill.

"Isn't it lovely, Mrs. C?" They stood beside a Corinthian column, gazing at the Palladian-inspired room. An Italian marble floor gleamed beneath satin slippers and Wellington boots. The heaven-high ceiling was a study in ornate moldings and medallions. Gold-and-crystal chandeliers sparkled like stars, illuminating the bird's-egg blue walls. Giant palms embedded in huge Egyptian-style planters, situated at intervals on one side of the room, provided a screen for couples seeking privacy. And, at the opposite end of the cavernous chamber, tucked in a baroque little chancel, was a small orchestra desperately trying to make Handel audible above the din of gossip and laughter.

"Loverly, indeed." Mrs. Childress discreetly extracted a tiny bottle from her purse, poured a quantity of brandy in her punch, and tipped her cup again. "Much better," she admitted.

"You'd better be careful. Father and Dovie are here, you know. I don't know where, but they're probably spying on us this very minute."

"I think we gave them the slip the moment we pushed through the gaggle in the entrance hall."

"Don't underestimate Father."

Mrs. Childress gave a moue of skepticism. "You're the escape artist, dearie. Why do you think I've been treading on your heels ever since we arrived? Now, don't go and leave me again. My poor heart couldn't bear it."

Rosalind nodded sweetly at a passing couple whom she recognized as neighbors in Mayfair. With a fraudulent smile pasted on her lips, she said to Mrs. Childress, "Don't get drunk and pass out on me, then."

The nanny gasped and flinched with indignation, but Rosalind's gaze had already lit on someone else. Her pulse leapt as she studied the familiar profile, the prominent nose, the thick shock of dark hair. "He's here."

"I wasn't drunk last night on the beach."

"It's he." Rosalind's lips froze on the rim of her punch cup. Though her mouth was instantly parched, her stomach was too unsettled to countenance the bubbly concoction. Suddenly, the room seemed suffocatingly hot, the crowd unbearably close-knit. A wave of panic washed over her. "It can't be."

"I might have been a bit tipsy, but it was cold out there, and your silly stepmother didn't care a fig whether I froze me bloomin' limbs off—"

"Mrs. Childress, it's he!" Rosalind half turned and grasped her nanny's elbow.

The older woman's gaze followed Rosalind's. "Who is he?"

"Viscount Pershing, the man who kidnapped me last night! And that blond-headed fellow is one of his accomplices. I recognize him, I'm certain of it. Oh, Mrs. C., I feel a bit faint!"

"Here, have a taste of mine. The brandy helps."

Desperate, Rosalind took the cup from Mrs. Childress's hands, and gulped the fortified punch. A quick shudder was followed by a tingly warmth that oozed through her veins. Strangely, this fuzzy sensation was succeeded by an even warmer surge of courage. "I shall go and talk to him."

"Poppycock!"

Rosalind handed the cup back to Mrs. Childress, along with her own. "Look at me. Is my hair all mussed?"

"No, but—"

"Is my nose too shiny?"

"No, child."

"Is my neck mottled from excite—"

"Listen, Rosie!" Mrs. Childress waggled a finger in the air, but quickly changed her demeanor to one of false gaiety when a curious couple looked her way.

Though her lips curved upward, her whisper was full of steel. "I won't have you making a spectacle of yourself. You were right to say that Sir Sibbald and Lady Dovie are probably watching us this very minute. How will you explain your brazen behavior to them?"

"I'll tell them he was a total stranger and I wanted to meet him. I'll tell them—"

She stopped when she saw Mrs. Childress's eyes bulge and her gaze refocus. An odd presentiment slithered through her as her nanny's expression changed from one of stern disapprobation to outright fear. "Mrs. Childress, are you alright?"

The nanny's jowls quivered as her jaw fell slack. But, before she could answer, Rosalind felt the warmth of a strong male hand close around her bare elbow.

Turning, she met the darkly intense gaze of Rafe Lawless, Viscount Pershing. As his fingers released her arm, a phantom warmth simmered inside her. Heart hammering, she managed a weak smile and the very faintest of curtsies.

He smiled first at her, then at her chaperone. "Rafe Lawless, ma'am. Forgive me and my friend here for being so bold."

"And I'm Tom Wickham." Beneath a mop of golden curls, the man's face darkened. He extended his hand toward Mrs. Childress.

She placed an empty punch cup in his palm. "Sorry, somehow I wound up with two."

"Quite alright," he replied with a chuckle. "I've been known to be a two-handed drinker myself." After he had placed the cup on a passing servant's empty tray, Tom turned to Rosalind and gently squeezed her fingers.

Mrs. Childress eyed the men with suspicion, but introduced herself and her charge with utmost civility. Anyone watching would have thought the men spotted a pretty girl and took it upon themselves to meet her. With her nanny acting as chaperone, Rosalind was perfectly within the bounds of propriety. Unlike the night before.

"Do you live near here?" the viscount asked her.

"Most of the year, we live in London. But Father keeps a house in Brighton. More to satisfy my stepmother's need for a grand social life, I suspect." Rosalind felt the sharp look Mrs. Childress gave her. She shouldn't have criticized Lady Dovie and she knew it, but the truth was dangerously slippery when brandy was flowing through her veins.

"Don't you care for Brighton?" the viscount persisted.

Rosalind wished everyone else in the room would disappear. Self-conscious beneath the stares of Tom Wickham and Mrs. Childress, she replied, "It's a very pretty resort, but hardly a stimulating atmosphere. Look around. Everyone here is beautiful, but has anyone read a book of late? Does anyone here truly care a fig about the state of the government? When they discuss politics, it has more to do with Prinny's love life than whether Napoleon Bonaparte will make it to Moscow by Christmas. I don't mean to sound like a tedious blue-stocking, but—"

Mrs. Childress gasped. "Miss Yardley, you don't mean that!"

But the viscount laughed. "Well put, Miss Yardley. I couldn't agree more."

Tom Wickham chuckled, too. "As for me, I don't mind a vapid conversation every now and again! Too much seriousness is what bores me!"

At length, perhaps as much from nervousness as from amusement, Mrs. Childress joined in the laughter.

Emboldened, Rosalind said, "And where do you hale from, Lord Pershing?"

His eyes glimmered at the pretense of their not knowing one another. "I have a house near Rye. Perched on a cliff overlooking the ocean, actually. It's really quite gothic, especially when the wind blows and the entire place creaks like a ship being tossed by a tempest."

"Near Rye? Tell me, did you see the bonfires at Hastings last night?"

His gaze was penetrating. "No."

"Too bad. They were beautiful, weren't they, Mrs. Childress?"

The nanny gave her a tight-lipped nod.

Rosalind felt a pinch of mischief. "And might I ask what you do—for a living, that is?"

Looking as if she where about to faint, Mrs. Childress said, "Child, what is the matter with you? 'Tis impolite to ask a gentleman what he does for a living! Why, I'm sure he does, er, *nothing* for a living!" The smile she gave the viscount was full of apology, as if Rosalind were a dim-witted child who couldn't be held accountable for her social gaffes.

The viscount's eyes twinkled. Clearly, he was enjoying this charade. "Mr. Wickham and I are in the shipping trade. Sugar, molasses, and rum from the Caribbean. That sort of thing."

"How very exotic. Is that all you ship?"

"Yes."

Rosalind was on the verge of asking another impertinent question when an aging woman, dressed in an old-fashioned corseted gown and wearing an alarming amount of white powder on her face, materialized. Dovie's description of Lady Toppainsley, right down to the little beauty mark pasted near the corner of her lips, was absurdly accurate.

Rafe made a handsome leg, while Tom Wickham executed a rather clumsy bow. The men introduced themselves, then the viscount smoothly presented Miss Rosalind Yardley and her governess, Mrs. Childress.

The lady barely glanced at the nanny, but gave Rosalind a scalding appraisal from head to toe. "Sir Sibbald's girl! Dovie told me you were a pretty thing, but who ever believes a word she says?"

As tiresome as Dovie was, Rosalind rankled at this lady's barbed remark. "My stepmother was certainly accurate in her description of you, my lady. You have an ageless beauty."

Tom Wickham coughed behind his gloved hand. Mrs. Childress anxiously sipped her punch, and the viscount, smiling broadly, quickly interceded.

"Thank you for inviting Mr. Wickham and me to your party." As Lord Pershing drew the lady's attention, her gaze softened. "It promises to be the *soiree* of the season, judging from the looks of it."

The lady's smile revealed rows of smallish teeth, yellow against her pale face powder. The air of decay and decadence surrounding her made Rosalind's skin prickle. "You were invited for a reason, Lord Pershing. My husband wants to meet you."

The viscount's thick brows arched. "I am honored."

"And curious, I reckon." The older woman's laugh sounded like a cat attempting to dislodge a hairball. "As well you should be. But, you see, my husband has made inquiries regarding the ocean front property on which your house is situated. When he learned who owned the property, he inquired about you. You're quite a legend in these parts, Lord Pershing. I must admit, my curiosity was piqued as well."

"I assure you, I've done nothing to earn such notoriety. I keep to myself as much as possible. Perhaps that is why the local folk speculate so. I wouldn't believe a word of what you hear, my lady. I'm actually quite the recluse."

"Just so." The lady's gaze took in the viscount's entire figure, from his polished boots to his snug buff-colored breeches to his thick wavy hair. Jealousy poured through Rosalind's veins, but she stood stock-still, feeling very young and out of her depth. "The town folk in Rye say you are rarely seen at social gatherings. Since your wife's death, you've practically given all of society the cut direct. To your credit, your name hasn't been linked in scandal to a single young lady since you became a widower! 'Struth, I expected you to be an ugly, bitter man, my lord."

"I'm not bitter."

The old tabby purred. "You're not ugly, either."

Rosalind couldn't bear it any longer. "Would you like to dance, Lord Pershing?"

"Only if they play a waltz," he replied.

"I'll go and make the request," Tom Wickham said, turning on his heel and quickly crossing the ballroom floor as if he couldn't wait to escape.

"Now there's a bold suggestion," Lady Toppainsley said. "Miss Yardley, if your nanny isn't going to say it, I suppose I am obliged. I do not believe your father would approve of your waltzing. Nothing personal, Lord Pershing."

"I'm sure not." The viscount half turned, gesturing toward the dance floor. "However, Miss Yardley is of the age of majority, if I am not mistaken. She is entitled to form her own opinions about what is appropriate conduct and what is not."

A frisson of excitement warmed Rosalind's cheeks. Yes, she was old enough to decide what was proper. And, right now, she deemed dancing with Rafe Lawless, Viscount Pershing, an entirely proper and wise course of action. Besides, it had the added appeal of irritating the devil out of Lady Toppainsley and shocking poor old Mrs. Childress.

She placed her hand in the viscount's proffered palm. True to his word, Tom Wickham had persuaded the orchestra to play a waltz. A buzz of restlessness filled the room, and the dance floor filled with couples eager to defy convention. Rosalind felt as if she were gliding on air.

Lord Pershing wondered if he had lost his mind. As

Rosalind's fingers clutched his hand, a burning desire to hold her in his arms overwhelmed his reason. In some dim recess of his consciousness, he was aware that waltzing with Sir Sibbald's daughter was a risky proposition. He was inviting scrutiny and disapprobation upon himself; he was begging the country's leading anti-smuggling zealot to despise him.

Yet, he couldn't refuse the young woman a dance. She'd wanted desperately to rid herself of her chaperone's watchfulness, if only for a few minutes. Her frustration was as clear as the pretty little *retroussé* nose on her face. Her brazen request for a waltz amused him. Her warm, lithe body in his arms aroused him. He wondered if she had any idea the effect she had on him.

She fit snugly against him, her limbs brushing against his as they moved across the floor. "You're a wonderful dancer." He felt her figure in his embrace, the tiny width of her waist, the firmness of her middle.

"Thank you for rescuing me from that simpering old Lady Toppainsley." She half-frowned, a twinkle of mischief in her gaze.

Sighing, he scanned the rows of onlookers. Some appeared stunned, some bemused as they watched the younger couples waltz. He knew that somewhere in that crowd was Sir Sibbald Yardley, eyeing his daughter like a hawk. "I don't know that I've rescued you from anything, dear. Your father might be even more disapproving than Lady Toppainsley. Aren't you growing weary of trying his patience?"

"I'm growing weary of his impatience."

"How did you explain your disappearance last night?"

"I told him I got lost on the beach, tripped over a rock, and fell down. I fainted, woke up this morning, walked to the road, and flagged down a carriage that was heading toward Brighton."

"That's an impossible fabrication!" Rafe felt a sudden quickening of his pulse. This little minx was a rotten liar; her father surely knew it. In fact, Sir Sibbald was probably glaring suspiciously at Rafe right now. "Did your father not threaten to dispatch you to a nunnery?"

"Hardly. He might have been a bit suspicious, but he chose to believe me. What choice did he have? I wasn't hurt—"

Her coolness unnerved Rafe. "Your gown wasn't even damp. How could you have spent the night on the beach?"

"He was relieved to see me walk in the door. I don't think he wanted to know the truth."

"I don't believe you." Rafe met her periwinkle gaze. Her wide-eyed innocence was enough to make any man, even the most jaded, want to believe her. Her charm was frightening. He imagined Sir Sibbald listening to his daughter's preposterous story, looking into her guileless expression, and concluding that she was incapable of deception. *Despite the fact that her explanation didn't fit the evidence at all.* "Well, perhaps you do have your father wrapped around your little finger. But, give him a little time, and he'll begin pressing you as to your whereabouts."

"I shall not deviate from my story."

He chuckled. "Like any good little criminal. Just see that you don't, Rosalind."

She pressed herself more snugly to his body, angling herself so that her head was level with his right shoulder. He fought the urge to wrap his arms completely around her; his hand on the small of her back was sufficient contact to send arrows of flame shooting through his body.

But it seemed so natural to want her to snuggle against the crook of his neck. She was as soft and alluring as a kitten, as dangerously erotic as a tigress.

Inhaling, the viscount detected soap and a vague floral aroma, the clean smell of her thick hair, the feminine perfume of her skin. Rosalind clung to him, and as they whirled about the floor, he gazed at her slender neck, her creamy skin, the hint of cleavage peeping from her Empress-waist gown. Miss Rosalind Yardley was a fascinating creature, he concluded, high-spirited and on the verge of womanhood. But was she merely testing the waters, seeking adventure, romance, and release from the confinement of her father's values . . . or was she prepared to be in love?

Annette's face, so pretty even after illness had hollowed her cheeks and darkened her eyes, haunted Rafe's thoughts. She'd been so energetic when he first met her, so eager to sample life's pleasures. Against her father's will, she married a Corinthian buck who took her to far-flung corners of the world, and introduced her to a life she'd never have known had she remained sequestered in the ivory tower her father had constructed for her. But, in the end, Annette had been more suited for her father's world. And she'd resented Rafe for taking her away.

He supposed that Miss Rosalind Yardley would also, in time. Best to leave her where she was, then. Best not to trifle with her affections. Best to protect himself against her ample charms.

"People are staring." He pushed her away a bit, creating more distance between them.

"I don't care."

"You will. Someday."

Her brow wrinkled. "You said I was old enough to decide for myself what was proper behavior."

"The fact you are old enough does not mean you are exercising good judgment."

Her eyes snapped, and her body tensed in his embrace. "Are you questioning my judgment?"

In truth, he was questioning her maturity, but he didn't dare admit that to her. "I am suggesting that you consider the consequences of your actions. The top-lofty old tabbies can be extraordinarily cruel, especially to pretty young innocents such as yourself. Don't ruin your reputation over me, dear."

"It's just a dance, my lord."

Rafe made an elegant turn, and guided Rosalind toward the orchestra end of the room. Over her head, he gave the room a quick, scathing search. Lady Toppainsley, and her husband, presumably, along with Mrs. Childress and the Yardleys had formed a little huddle on the other end of the room. Sir Sibbald lifted his head to stare at his daughter and her dance partner. A streak of defiance, and perhaps an element of hot desire, plumed outward from his heart. Deftly, he whirled Rosalind behind a screen of potted plants, and for a moment they were protected from view.

"So you think this is merely a dance, Rosalind?" He lowered his head, and gave her a quick hard kiss on the lips.

She gasped. Lashes fluttering, cheeks scarlet, she clung to his hand and shoulder like ivy.

He drew her more closely into his embrace, and as he waltzed her down the length of miniature palms, whispered in her ear, "The waltz may seem an innocuous dance, dear, but those who oppose it know how erotic it can be. Your body fitted snugly against mine . . . my thigh pressed between your legs . . . like this."

"Oh!" Her head tilted back as he parted her thighs with his own, slipping his booted foot between her satin slippers, moving with her and against her and whirling her around beneath the sparkling chandeliers.

"You like it. You know you do." Seeing the look of helplessness in Rosalind's rounded eyes, he felt a surge of wanton hunger. Sir Sibbald be damned! The girl in Rafe's arms was aching to be released from her tight little corset of a world. And he was just the man to free her. He thought he might be crazy; his attraction to Rosalind could only be ill-fated. They had no future, he and this pampered little virgin. Yet, she clung to him as if he were her only hope.

A tocsin rang in his head. He didn't want to be any woman's *only hope.* He'd been Annette's only hope to escape from her tyrannical father, hadn't he? And, though he'd loved Annette dearly, the pressure of trying to make amends to her had nearly driven him insane. And, in the end, he felt he never made her happy.

He would never make Miss Rosalind Yardley happy. Not in the long run. So, why was he trifling with her affections now? What sort of twisted, evil impulse was he acting on? Why couldn't he, the older and wiser of the two, exercise his own good judgment and return her to her father's custody right now?

"Kiss me," she whispered, staring up at him. "Kiss me again. Please. Quickly! Before we are back on the dance floor. Before anyone sees us!"

The world crashed in on her like a meteor flung from the heavens. As they smoothly rejoined the couples on the dance floor, Rosalind and Rafe held each other at a respectable distance, their limbs disengaged from one another's, their bodies parting. Her lips burned from the harsh intensity of Rafe's kiss. Her body ached for a closer joinder with his.

"Don't worry." His voice was thick and throaty. "No one saw."

She prayed no one had. The very notion someone might have spied them kissing behind the potted palms sent a jolt of fear up her spine. But, Rosalind thought, she'd have taken the risk anyway. The thrill of being kissed by Rafe was worth it.

The imprint of his lips on hers still tingled. But, as he waltzed her the length of the room, her knees slowly lost their wobble, and her pulse slowed. By the time they came into view of Sir Sibbald and his little congregation, Rosalind had regained much of her composure.

When they were within ten paces of her father, Rosalind noted his stern expression. "Don't mind Father," she warned the viscount. "He may seem a bit gruff, but he's actually . . ."

"He's actually more than a bit gruff," Rafe interjected. "He could have me dancing in the air with a stroke of his pen."

"He wouldn't."

The music ended. Rosalind and Rafe came to a standstill, then shook hands politely and thanked one another for the dance. The viscount led her back to her father, and gave a dignified bow to the man whose daughter he'd kissed behind the screen of potted plants.

Introductions seemed beside the point. "Thank you for allowing me to dance with your daughter, Sir Sibbald."

The man's peregrine eyes focused on Rafe. "Lady Toppainsley tells me you are the viscount who owns that old mansion perched on the ledge outside Rye."

Rafe met Sir Sibbald's gaze. "There seems to be much interest in my property of late. Given the dilapidated condition of my house, I confess I am at a loss as to understand why."

Tension crackled between the two men. A moment of silence stretched while Lady Dovie put her arm protectively around Rosalind's waist.

Glancing at Mrs. Childress, Rosalind saw that the nanny was sipping her punch heavily and looking distraught. The Toppainsleys, Lord and Lady, stood rigidly, studiously observing Sir Sibbald's encounter with Lord Pershing. In their period costumes and powdered wigs, they looked like they'd just stepped out of the previous century. Queasiness washed over Rosalind as she sensed the hostility brewing beneath the surface of this tableau.

"There is a flurry of smuggling going on in that area," Sir Sibbald said.

"The entire coastal area is a hotbed of smuggling activity." Rafe didn't blink.

"My daughter may have told you who I am, and that I have been commissioned by the King's Bench to investigate the illegal importation of brandy, wine, and other French contraband."

"She didn't mention it, but I am pleased to hear it. I wish you the best of luck in your endeavors."

Sir Sibbald hesitated, obviously attempting to judge Rafe's tone. Was the viscount mocking him? "Your property is in the perfect location to establish a central headquarters. For my investigation, that is."

"I'm afraid I'm not interested in selling," Lord Pershing replied. "The house was built by my father. It may be falling down around my ears, but it has sentimental value to me."

"Pish-posh!" Lady Toppainsley's smile looked like it had been carved in a jack-o'-lantern. "Anyone will sell if the price is right."

The viscount's smile was more akin to Mona Lisa's. "My house and I are not for sale."

The lady's smile faded and her lashes fluttered. Beneath a heavy layer of pale makeup, her cheeks darkened. "You would do well to watch your tongue—"

"Now, now, Valdosta!" Lord Toppainsley patted the air with his hands. His droopy silver moustache lent a sleepy look to his expression, but his watery blue eyes were full of bristle. "I'm sure the viscount meant no insult. Did you, old man? Of course not! And just to prove there's no hard feelings, why don't you attend dinner with us this Saturday evening? Valdosta and I are planning a small party, just the Yardleys and ourselves. We'd be pleased if you would join us."

Lady Dovie couldn't suppress her surprise. "Are we having dinner with you on Saturday? I didn't know—"

Sir Sibbald cut her off. "You must have forgot, dear. With all those calling cards and invitations piled on the tray in the foyer, I'm hardly surprised."

"Of course, we expect Miss Rosalind to be there, too," warbled Lady Toppainsley.

Rosalind felt as if someone had punched her in the ribs. Her chest ached from the pounding her heart had given it. Glancing at Rafe, she saw the indecision in his expression. Silently, she begged him to decline the Toppainsley's invitation. If she had to face him across a dinner table, she was quite certain she would make a fool of herself. On the other hand, if he turned down the invitation, Rosalind would be shattered.

His dark gaze locked with hers. "In that case, how can I say no?"

"Bring your Mr. Wickham, too," Lord Toppainsley added. "He seems like a right funny fellow."

"Will do. And now, if you'll excuse me, it's getting rather late—" The viscount politely smiled at everyone in the little group. His expression altered when he looked at Mrs. Childress.

Rosalind, hardly able to tear her gaze from his broad shoulders and handsome face, half turned in time to see Mrs. Childress's eyes roll back in her head. The Yardleys and the Toppainsleys stared in shock as the governess's head tilted oddly. Her cup slipped from her fingers and crashed to the floor. Her knees seemed to crumple beneath the weight of her body. Just before Mrs. Childress hit the floor, Lord Pershing caught her in his arms.

Six

In the dimly lit corridor outside Mrs. Childress's bedchamber, Lady Dovie and Rosalind stood waiting. When the surgeon emerged, closing the door quietly behind him, his face was grim.

"Poison," the man said. "She's a strong old battle-ax, though. A good night's sleep and she'll be good as new."

"Poison?" echoed Lady Dovie. "But who would do such a thing?"

A chill floated through Rosalind as she recalled passing her punch cup to Mrs. Childress. Was it possible that someone had tried to poison *her*, and she had unwittingly given the poison to her governess?

"I must see her," Rosalind murmured, brushing past the doctor.

"She needs her rest," warned the man. "I wouldn't expect too much from her."

Inside the bedchamber, a small taper burned beside Mrs. Childress's bed, casting an eerie glow on the woman's pasty face. Flat on her back, hands folded neatly across her chest, she appeared as lifeless as a corpse. Guilt muffled Rosalind's thudding heart as she crossed the floor and stood beside her governess's bed. Had she inadvertently injured her beloved nanny, just hours after she'd mistakenly shot an innocent man?

Tears streamed down her cheeks. "I'm so sorry," she managed to whisper.

"For what, gel?" Mrs. Childress asked as her eyes opened.

Startled, Rosalind clutched the older woman's hand. "For giving you the poison."

"So, it was you who tried to poison me?"

"No, of course not!"

"I didn't think so. Then why are you apologizing?" Though Mrs. Childress's grip was weak, and her flesh cold, her eyes held a twinkle of warmth.

"The poison must have been in my cup. I must have given it to you."

"Poppycock. I drank too much. Got a bad dose of brandy, that's all. Can't count on the quality of the stuff when you have to depend on bootleggers and pirates to get it for you."

Rosalind wiped her face with the sleeve of her dressing gown. "Is that where your brandy comes from, Mrs. C? From smugglers like Lord Pershing?"

"Mayhaps from Lord Pershing himself. Dearie, the little delivery boy who comes here is simply the middle man. I've never asked him who supplies his goods."

A sobering thought began to form in Rosalind's mind. Rather than worry her nanny, however, she leaned down and kissed the woman's cheek. "I'll see you in the morning." Slipping out of Mrs. Childress's room, she was surprised to see Lady Dovie still there, wringing her hands.

In the years since she'd come to live with them, Dovie hadn't appeared to care a fig about Mrs. Childress. Her worried look struck Rosalind as uncharacteristically genuine. Not for the first time in the last twenty-four hours, Rosalind was forced to look more closely at the people surrounding her, people whose emotions and loyalties she'd taken for granted—people whose motivations she had, perhaps, misjudged.

"She's going to be fine, Dovie. You can go to bed."

"I wish I could. I'll never sleep a wink. Do you really think someone poisoned her? And if they did so . . . why?"

Rosalind found herself in the awkward role of comforting Dovie. She linked her arm through Dovie's as they walked toward the staircase. "I wouldn't put too much stock in the what the doctor said. Father has always said he was a quack."

Dovie squeezed Rosalind's arm. "I have always suspected Mrs. C. was a drinker. Tell me, is it so?"

"You wouldn't expect me to tattle on my own nanny, now, would you?"

"Just as I thought," said Dovie. As the women stood on the landing, male voices floated up the carpeted steps. "Has she endangered her health?"

Rosalind hesitated, half listening to the voices belowstairs, half wondering whether Dovie's concern was a source of comfort or a cause for concern. "I don't think so. She takes a nip of brandy now and then. It helps her sleep. I've never known her to miss a day of work, or make herself sick from drinking."

"Your father would dismiss her without blinking an eye if he knew she so much as sipped a drop of liquor."

"I know." Rosalind froze, listening. The sound of men in earnest conversation drove all other thoughts from her mind. A deep velvety voice overlaid her father's stentorian tones. "Who is in the drawing room with Father?"

But, before Lady Dovie answered, Rosalind knew. The viscount's voice was as firmly embedded in her memory as the alphabet. His throaty chuckle was familiar; it brought to mind the scratch of his beard on her throat. She heard him say, "Rosalind," and her pulse galloped.

"That man, the one with whom you waltzed." Withdrawing her arm from Rosalind's, Lady Dovie gripped the banister. The two women descended the stairs quietly, both keenly aware of the male voices below. "You shouldn't have, you know."

"Shouldn't have waltzed with Lord Pershing?" Rosalind paused at the second landing. Tugging at the belt of her silk wrapper, she realized she was unpresentable. She'd be seeing no more of Viscount Pershing this night. Yet his voice was disturbing in its ability to arouse her. Frustrated, she frowned at Dovie. "Why ever not? 'Twas a totally innocent dance. Everyone was doing it."

" 'Everyone was doing it?' " Dovie mocked. "If everyone were throwing themselves off the London Bridge, I suppose you would do that also?"

Rosalind gave a little huff of exasperation. "Weren't you ever young, Dovie?"

The older woman drew herself up, obviously offended. "My dear, one does not have to be young to recognize the temptation of desire. Your feelings for the viscount are painfully clear, I assure you. Your Father was most displeased with your behavior tonight. Had it not been for Mrs. Childress's accident, and the chivalrous manner in which Lord Pershing assisted us home, I'm quite certain Sir Sibbald would have called the rapscallion out!"

"Called him out!"

Dovie's lashes fluttered. "Perhaps that is an exaggeration. But, Pershing should have known better than to seduce a green girl like you."

"Seduce? Green girl?" Rosalind's jaw fell slack.

"If a waltz isn't a seduction, I don't know what is."

Rosalind started to tell her stepmother that she knew the difference between a waltz and a seduction, but she held her tongue. No sense in fanning the flames of this debate, she told herself. At length, she said through clenched teeth, "I am not a green girl, Dovie."

"You're too young and inexperienced to defend yourself against the overtures of such a worldly—and admittedly handsome—man. Believe it or not, I was a young girl once. I know what you are thinking when you look at a man like that. And it's a dangerous thought, I can tell you."

It was far more dangerous than Dovie could ever know. But, the delicious thrill that accompanied it felt right. "It was just a waltz, Dovie. I am sorry if Father is angry with me."

"He would have cut in and demanded you leave the dance floor, but Mrs. Childress convinced him that a public reprimand would bring more attention to the situation. He didn't want to create a scandal."

"No, never a scandal."

"He decided to handle the matter in a more private manner."

"Yes, by all means, we should keep it under wraps."

"I'm certain the viscount will understand."

"Understand what?" Rosalind's throat constricted.

"That he is unsuitable for you. That he is not to dance with you, or court you, or have any sort of contact with you at all, other than the ordinary social discourse that might take place if he were to encounter you in public."

Anger bubbled in Rosalind's blood, but she managed to control the tautness in her voice. "If I run into him at the library, I may say hello. Is that it?"

Dovie eyed her suspiciously. "You will see him at the Toppainsley's dinner party on the weekend. You must speak politely with him, but if your Father senses any sort of flirtation between the two of you, it will not go well."

"Perhaps the viscount will not attend. Why should he? Father has insulted him beyond words. Why would Lord Pershing wish to spend his evening with a room full of stiff-rumped hypocrites?"

"Rosalind, watch your tongue."

"Will Father wash my mouth out with soap, too?"

"You'd be lucky if he didn't turn you over his knee,

if he were to hear such impertinent back-talk from you, young lady! Now, go to bed. Perhaps the excitement of the last few days has robbed you of your sense of decorum. I will give you the benefit of the doubt for tonight, but you'd best heed my advice where Lord Pershing is concerned. He's not for you, Rosie. Your father has decreed it. Defy him, and the consequences will be severe." Lady Dovie quickly continued downstairs.

Rosalind pivoted, her eyes stinging with hot tears. Stalking toward her room, she heard the sound of bootsteps emerging from the drawing room. She paused at the threshold of her bedchamber as a man's heavy tread descended the steps beneath her. The front door opened, then slammed shut, its heavy brass knocker rattling violently. An uncomfortable silence followed, reverberating throughout the house like canon shot.

Belowstairs, the muffled voices of Dovie and Sir Sibbald mingled in conspiratorial tones. A subtle click announced they had shuttered themselves behind closed doors, no doubt to gloat over their successful suppression of Rosalind's little insurrection.

Defeated, Rosalind threw herself on her bed. She'd been nothing but foolish, reckless, and irresponsible the last few days. She'd escaped the custody of her nanny only to fall into the clutches of a roguish smuggler. She'd kissed Lord Pershing in a way she supposed only a married woman should. She'd shot a man. She nearly killed Mrs. Childress. And now, she'd enraged her father by waltzing in public.

Somehow, waltzing in public didn't seem so terrible compared to the other sins she'd committed. Rosalind shuddered against her tear-stained pillow. An unbidden flood of heat poured through her body as she thought of Rafe's lips against hers. God only knew what Sir Sibbald would do if he ever found out how scandalously Rosalind had truly behaved.

She wished she could feel guilty about that.

But what she felt as she rolled onto her back, closed her eyes, and imagined Rafe's body pressed against hers, was definitely *not* guilt.

Rafe Lawless, Viscount Pershing, stood at the back door of a country inn midway between Brighton and Hastings. Scant starlight illuminated a dirty chicken yard patched with a crazy quilt of ice and debris. Agitated by his conversation with Sir Sibbald, Rafe banged his gloved fist on the flimsy door until, at length, a blink of candlelight appeared through the greasy glass panes.

The door swung open to reveal the pockmarked face of a man wearing nothing more than a striped nightshirt tucked into unbuttoned breeches. "What the devil are ye' wantin' at this ungodly hour?"

"I want my money."

The man scowled, but quickly scanned the chicken yard for signs of accomplices. "I done told your partner, I ain't got it. Business ain't been good of late. You'll have to wait."

"We're tired of waiting, Mr. Sawyer. In fact, we've extended you credit for well over six months, now. It's time to pay up."

"I don't have the money."

Rafe quickly took the two steps leading to the back door. Despite the man's bulky figure, he pushed past him into the combination storage room and kitchen. The smell of rotten food and grease hung heavily in the air, suggesting to Rafe that perhaps business at The Cockeyed Rooster wasn't as brisk as it should have been. "Where do you keep your money?"

The man's tallow taper sputtered in protest. "I told you, I haven't got any money. You'd better leave now, Pershing, or—"

"Or what? You'll report me to the authorities? Go right ahead, Mr. Sawyer. I'm certain they would be very interested in your complaint. Now, tell me where your money is, or I'll be forced to find it myself. Even if that means turning this inn upside down, and waking every guest in the house."

The man hesitated, judging his chances of escaping payment to his liquor vendor, wondering if Pershing was serious about searching his inn for money. Rafe's withdrawal of a small pistol ended the man's internal debate. Staring at the gun's snout, he stammered, "In the chamber pot beneath me wife's bed. I'll go and get it."

"I'll go with you."

"She's not decent!"

"I won't look." Rafe gave the man a chilling smile, then followed him up the back stairs till they reached the third floor of the inn. Bare floorboards creaked beneath their feet as they made their way down a cold passageway. Somewhere belowstairs, a guest could be heard snoring. A piquant perfume of unwashed bodies, unlaundered linens and unemptied chamber pots prickled the viscount's nose.

Mr. Sawyer paused before a closed door. "I'll go in and get what money I've hidden away. You stay here."

"I'll go with you."

"I told you, my wife—"

"Judging from these indelicate surroundings, I doubt her sensibilities will be offended by the presence of a man in her bedchamber."

Sawyer's scowl deepened, but he pushed open the door, and crossed the threshold. Through a badly smeared window, starlight bathed the room in an eerie glow. Pinching his nose, Rafe scanned the sparse furnishings. A wooden four-poster bed, piled with quilts and counterpanes, dominated the tiny room. As Sawyer approached it, there emerged a heavy sigh from beneath the covers. Edging closer to the foot of the bed, Rafe thought that if Mrs. Sawyer's housekeeping reflected her physical state of being, he had little desire to see her in any degree of *dishabille*. Instinctively, he kept his distance.

"It's alright, Pru, go back to sleep."

"Who is it?" asked a grumpy voice.

Sawyer placed his taper on a rickety table, squatted, then reached beneath the bed. "Just a bill collector, dearie. Nothing to worry your pretty little head over."

The scrape of a chamber pot on the wooden floor caused the figure beneath the bedclothes to stir. "No money there," the gravelly voice replied.

"I done told him that, dear. But, he insists on seeing where we stash our money."

The voice beneath the pillows was groggy. "Don't give him any. His liquor was no count anyhow."

Sawyer remained on his haunches, his hands beneath the low frame of the bed. Rafe's senses suddenly clanged with awareness. Sawyer's wife, if that's who she was, mentioned the quality of Rafe's liquor. But Sawyer had said the interloper in their bedchamber was a bill collector. How did a woman, disturbed in her sleep, figure out that Rafe was really—

Sawyer's quick movements belied his bulky form. A shotgun swung up from beneath the bed, its long double barrels pointing directly at Rafe's chest. Clutching the gun's stock to his chest, Sawyer slowly rose. "Put the pistol down, my lord."

The lumpy figure in the bed rolled over and sat up, revealing the pock-marked face of an old woman. "Shoot him, that's what I say." Rafe dropped the pistol he held in his hand.

"Shoot him," Mrs. Sawyer growled. "Ain't that what the gent told you—"

"Hush your mouth, old woman!" Sawyer cut his wife a quelling gaze, but quickly looked back at Rafe. "I don't want to have to blow yer head off, m'lord. But I will if I haf'ta."

"You'll have to kill me, Sawyer. Otherwise, I'll come back some day when you're not expecting me, and I'll take every penny you've got in your house. I'll take what's left of my inventory back, too. Perhaps I'll rob the pockets of every guest in your inn. One way or another, I'll get what you owe me. I have to, you see. If I let you get away without paying me, my other customers will think they can do the same. It's business, Sawyer."

"Aye, it's business, Pershing. But, I'm doing business with someone else, now. Don't want no more of your rotten liquor—"

"I've never sold you bad liquor, Sawyer. You know that."

"Shoot him!" the hag in the bed cried.

"Who's been cutting in on my territory?" Pershing demanded.

Sawyer lifted the shotgun to his shoulder and stared down the barrel. At this range, if he pulled the trigger, it would be more than Rafe's head that would be blown off. Instinctively, Rafe took a step back, reaching behind for the pistol he kept tucked in the waistband of his breeches, the very pistol that Rosalind had pilfered from him a few nights earlier. He rarely traveled without at least two weapons hidden on his body, readily available in the event he was ambushed or attacked. After all, he was in the business of smuggling; it was, by its nature, a hazardous occupation.

In the dim, sputtering candlelight, Rafe saw Sawyer's fingers flex and tighten around the shotgun's trigger case. Lightning quick, Rafe whipped his pistol out, pointed it at Sawyer and fired.

The report from the pistol was a loud pop! The returning shotgun blast was a deafening thunderclap.

Rafe dove toward the door as plaster exploded in the wall behind him. Mrs. Sawyer screamed obscenities and her husband fired again. This time, the door

frame shattered as Rafe ran through it. Footsteps
sounded behind him, and he zigzagged down the
dark corridor as Sawyer, having quickly and expertly
reloaded his weapon, came into the hallway and fired
again.

Half running, half leaping down the back staircase,
Rafe heard the cries and shouts of confused, frightened guests as the inn erupted in a hail of shotgun
pellets. He made it out the back door and jumped
onto the back of his horse just as Sawyer spilled into
the chicken yard behind him. Ducking, Rafe urged
the animal to a sturdy gallop, and was on the rutted
road to Hastings within an instant.

After a minute or so of hard running, Rafe slowed
his horse to a more comfortable pace. Sawyer hadn't
pursued him, and most likely wouldn't. He'd shot at
Rafe, but he hadn't killed him, and in Rafe's opinion,
hadn't tried very diligently to do so. Sawyer wouldn't
expect Rafe to return, and so, having refused to pay
for liquor he'd already resold to customers, he'd ac-
complished what he'd set out to do.

What Sawyer couldn't know was that Rafe had no
intention of fading away. Mrs. Sawyer's enigmatic re-
marks required redress. And Rafe wouldn't rest easily
until he figured out what had really happened at The
Cockeyed Rooster Inn tonight.

A few hours later, Rafe sat at his favorite table in
the corner at the rear of The Salty Dog. Across from
him sat Tom Wickham, bleary eyed and pale.

"No one wanted to pay," Tom complained around a mouthful of sausage.

The proprietor of the tavern had obliged the men with a hearty repast of eggs, biscuits, and thick country sausages. Rafe had eaten heartily and now sat sipping a cup of steaming Turkish coffee. Since his travels had introduced him to the pleasures of the strong, harsh brew, he'd given up the traditional English habit of drinking tea. "There's something afoot," he agreed, pinching the bridge of his nose. "Sawyer knew I was coming. If it hadn't been for his wife's slip of the tongue, he'd have blown my head off. I was lucky this time, Tom, but who knows what could happen the next time . . ."

"You weren't lucky, Rafe. You're not a lucky man. You were quick and you were smart and you were too intelligent by far to fall into the trap Sawyer set for you."

Rafe sighed. "This damnable business is getting a mite dangerous."

"It was always dangerous." Tom stared curiously at his closest friend and business partner. "You've never seemed to mind that it was. In fact, I've often thought you relished the danger, invited it, even."

The proprietor of the inn set a fresh cup of coffee in front of Rafe. As he stirred a spoonful of sugar into the black liquid, and squeezed a wedge of lemon over the slightly oily surface, he felt a sharp twist of his gut.

Tom was right; he had recklessly invited danger upon his head more than once. Too many close brushes with the authorities, too many voyages in bad weather, and too many deliveries of contraband liquor to unsavory characters in places of ill repute, had imbued him with a sense of invincibility. It was a wonder he hadn't had his throat sliced open by a double-crossing customer, or been hung by the likes of Sir Sibbald Yardley. It was a miracle Rafe Lawless was still alive.

He wasn't invincible, though. He'd been tweaking the nose of fate ever since Annette died. Grief had made him numb, even to danger. The only sensation he had felt in the past five years was his audacious flirtation with death, and even that had lately lost its excitement.

What did excite him? What could?

Unbidden, the image of Miss Rosalind Yardley floated across Rafe's mind. *She* excited him. The hold she had on his attention was tighter than a barnacle's grip on a rotting hull. Ever since he'd kissed her, he hadn't been able to dismiss her from his thoughts.

"Rafe?" Tom's voice intruded on the viscount's imaginings. "Are you alright?"

He wasn't, but he wasn't going to admit to any weakness. "What's going on, Tom? Why aren't our customers paying? Why did Sawyer try to kill me?"

"Who set you up, Rafe? That's the question. Someone told Sawyer you were coming, and he was ready for you."

"No one knew I was going to The Cockeyed Rooster Inn tonight." Rafe gulped his beer. "No one except you."

"Are you certain?"

A jab of pain pierced Rafe's stomach. "Yes. Good

God, how could they have? I didn't decide myself until tonight, while we were standing around at that horrid soiree. You were right there with me, next to the orchestra, when we discussed it."

Tom nodded. "Perhaps someone overheard it."

The thought occurred to Rafe at the same instant. "We were standing in front of that ridiculous row of potted palms."

"Ah, the decorative tropical jungle that screened you and Miss Yardley from the rest of the dance floor."

"You were aware of what I was doing?" Rafe couldn't suppress a crooked smile.

"The thickest imbecile in the room could have figured out what you were doing, old man. And it didn't help that Miss Yardley had a decidedly guilty look on her face when the two of you finally emerged, waltzing from behind the ramparts as if Cupid himself were flinging arrows at your hearts."

"Christ on a raft! Was it that obvious, Tom?"

"Her cheeks were pink, her little bosom was heaving, her eyes were all aglow with emotion—"

"Oh God, spare me! You sound like one of those torrid romance novelists."

"Did her father give you an upbraiding? After Mrs. Childress was pronounced fit for duty, that is?"

"That's putting it mildly." Rafe cringed at the harsh words Sir Sibbald had used. If any other man had talked to him in such imperious tones, he would have challenged him to a duel, right then and there. But, the man was Rosalind's father, and for some strange reason, Rafe allowed him some quarter for his over-reactions. After all, Rafe thought, if Rosalind were his daughter, the thought of another man wanting her would drive him insane, too. Odd that he would have such sympathy for a man who had the power to ruin his life.

"He told me to leave her alone. Told me in no uncertain terms that if I didn't, I would live to regret it."

Tom pushed his empty plate aside. "That's it then, Rafe. You must leave her alone. If you don't, you're inviting the scrutiny of one of the most dangerous men in England. To us, anyway. The last thing we need right now is Sir Sibbald breathing down our necks. Especially now. Someone has got it in for us, Rafe, and we've got to watch our backs more carefully than ever."

"You don't think Sir Sibbald has anything to do with last night, do you, Tom?"

"I don't see how he could." Tom scratched the top of his head. "But, we mustn't take any chances, Rafe. Stay away from that girl."

Something rankled about being warned off Rosalind Yardley. "She isn't a girl. She's a fully grown woman with a mind of her own. And I've a right to see whom I please. And socialize with whom I please."

"Not this girl, Rafe," Tom said through clenched teeth.

"It's going to be damned awkward seeing her at the Toppainsley's dinner party—"

"What dinner party?"

"You're invited, by the way." A flash of anger

heated Rafe's emotions. "And, how am I supposed to act toward Rosalind? As if she's too good for me, too aristocratic, too refined and fragile and precious for the likes of me? Am I to fetch her champagne and entertain her with clever banter while she waits for a more suitable man, a more acceptable husband, to happen along? Am I to pretend I have no real interest in her?"

"Jesus, Rafe, I didn't realize you were so bitter. You've never forgiven Annette's father, have you?"

Rafe slammed his fist on the table. "I've never forgiven *myself!* I should have called that weasel of a man out and put a bullet through his hard little heart the first time he told me to stay away from Annette. But, I didn't, you see. I didn't! I didn't want to hurt *her.*" Rafe's head fell heavily into his open palms, fingers clutching at his throbbing temples. "I thought when he saw how dearly I loved her, he would forgive me for what I was."

At length, Tom said quietly, "You were a good man, Rafe. There was nothing to forgive."

"I held an inferior title, and I dared to dirty my hands with commerce. Annette's father nearly fainted when he heard I was in the shipping business. I suppose if he discovered I began smuggling liquor after Annette died, he would be immensely gratified. It would prove his theory that I was a lesser man than he. It would validate his belief that I never was good enough for Annette."

The proprietor of the inn glanced over from the long mahogany bar which he methodically wiped with a damp towel. When he looked away, Tom reached across the table and squeezed his friend's shoulder. "You're having a rough patch. Things will get better."

Rafe rubbed his face with his hands. He was mortified that he'd shown such emotion, and grateful that it was Tom who'd witnessed his vulnerability. But, even his dearest friend couldn't understand how he felt. The bitter anger Rafe had nurtured for the past five years was eating away at the foundation of his existence in the same way the wind and saltwater slowly eroded the framework of his house on the cliff. He knew that his criminal activity, and his embrace of danger, was a reckless, defiant reaction to his grief. He knew he was slowly killing himself. He thought he should have blown his head off long ago, or leapt off a ship's bow into the ocean. The result would have been the same; the end would simply have come more quickly.

But, competing with his desire for self-destruction was now a disturbingly novel emotion. For the first time in five years, Rafe had felt something. Something other than grief and loneliness. And it had been a good feeling, one that made him suddenly hungry for life. His blood had run hot and his loins had tingled; but that wasn't all he'd felt when he'd been with Rosalind. He thought he'd absorbed a bit of her youthful optimism; for a short time, his cynicism had faded away. For a short time, he'd believed that life was sweet and happiness possible.

Then, when her father told him to stay away from her, when Rafe realized he'd been forever stricken from Rosalind's world, that incredible feeling of lightness vanished. His grief returned.

Now, everything he held in his hands was emptiness. His fingers craved the silkiness of Rosalind's skin. His lips burned to kiss hers. Worse, his heart craved the comfort that her tender arms had offered him.

It didn't matter, though. Rafe had no intention of repeating his past mistake. Rosalind's father was right; the girl needed a different sort of man than he. Rafe would do her a favor by keeping his distance.

When he looked up, Tom was staring at him with grave concern. Giving a final boot-kick to his emotions, Rafe stood. "Don't worry, old man, I have no intention of riling Sir Sibbald's anger. I quite agree, we don't need him as an enemy."

"It's just that I would hate to see you . . ." For once, Tom searched for a word. "Hurt."

A bitter bark of laughter escaped Rafe's lips. "Didn't you just say I wasn't lucky, but rather too smart to fall into the Sawyers' trap. What makes you think I'll fall into Sir Sibbald's trap?"

"That's not the trap I'm worried about, Rafe."

Rafe half turned toward the door, eager now to escape his friend's mother-hen concern. He'd done quite enough soul-searching for today. He'd made his decision regarding Rosalind and it was final. He was, after all, a man of action, and not one inclined to sit around and contemplate his feelings and emotions.

Tom followed him toward the tavern's front door. But, both men drew up short when they saw a young woman emerge from a rented carriage standing in the road just outside.

"Is that—" Rafe instinctively took a step backward. "Tom, are my eyes playing tricks on me?"

"If they are, mine are equally unreliable," answered Tom, retreating. "What in the devil would Miss Rosalind Yardley be doing here?"

"I don't know." Rafe and Tom pivoted. "But I intend to find out. Come on, we can listen from the kitchen."

They slipped though the galley doors that separated the kitchen from the bar, nodding conspiratorially at the proprietor. The man's gaze cut from their departing backs to the door. As it opened, the lintel bell tinkled brightly. If the tavern owner was curious as to why Rafe and Tom would care to eavesdrop on another of his customers, his expression didn't reveal it. Instead, he continued mopping his bar, while offering a pleasant smile to the young lady who'd just entered his establishment.

"What can I get for you this morning, ma'am?"

She was a pretty girl, with beautiful pale blue eyes and raven hair. "Can you pour me a cup of tea?" she asked sweetly.

She sat at the table recently vacated by Rafe and Tom. The proprietor wasted little time in furnishing her a pot of hot tea and a tiny plate of biscuits. He was turning back to his bar when she asked him a strange question.

"Do you know a man named Redd Fellowes?"

Seven

She hadn't even drunk a proper cup of tea before her business at The Salty Dog was concluded. The proprietor there claimed ignorance not only of Redd Fellowes, but also of any smuggling activity near Hastings, Brighton, Rye, or for that matter, all of England. If you'd believed the man, you'd have thought no one in the British Empire had sipped a drop of Bordeaux wine since Bonaparte had seized power.

Stepping onto the cobbled street, Rosalind pulled her cloak more tightly about her neck. Her driver lumbered from his seat and placed a tiny step beneath the carriage door. As Rosalind lifted her skirts off the rain-slicked road, she thought she'd wasted her morning and gone to an awful lot of trouble for naught. Sneaking out of the house while Dovie thought she was sleeping hadn't been a simple feat. And, if she didn't get back soon, someone would find her bed empty and another search party would be dispatched to hunt her down.

"Miss Yardley?" The deep male voice came from

behind, startling her so that her half-boot slipped off the step and she lost her balance.

Instantly, he was at her side, grasping her elbow. "Forgive me, I didn't mean to frighten you." He slipped a coin to the driver, and said, "We'll sit inside the carriage for a moment. Don't set off just now."

"Where did you come from?" Rosalind allowed the viscount to help her settle on the hard leather squab, beneath a thick lap blanket. She thought he released her arm rather reluctantly, before sitting opposite her and removing his beaver hat. Absently rubbing her ankle, she stared at him, surprised by the rough growth of bristle on his jaw and the purple shading beneath his eyes. "You look as if you haven't slept a wink."

"I confess I haven't made it to my bed as yet. After I left your father's house, I ran Tom to ground. It wasn't too difficult to find a disreputable club and a dangerous card game to lose ourselves in." When he smiled, the wrinkles at the corners of his eyes deepened.

He looked older today than he had the day before, Rosalind thought. "Dovie told me that Father warned you off."

He pushed back against the leather cushion, his gaze boring into hers, his fingers working the brim of his hat. "You're too dear for me, it seems. Or, perhaps, too young."

"I thought we'd firmly established that I was sufficiently old to make my own decisions."

His lips curved. "We agree on that point, Miss

Yardley. Your father does not. And he is responsible for your welfare."

"I am responsible for myself." Despite the chill inside the carriage, Rosalind felt a surge of warmth. "You can see I am an independent woman. I'm here without a chaperone, aren't I? How many women—"

"Very few." His voice was taut, sending a little shock through Rosalind's system. "Which begs the question. What are you doing in a greasy tavern, alone, at this time of the morning?"

"I wanted a beer."

"That's a bloody lie."

"I'll remind you to watch your language!"

He appeared to bite back another harsh remark. Instead, he said through clenched teeth, "How did you sneak away without an escort? What would your father do if he knew what you were about?"

"The same thing he'd do if he knew what went on in your carriage a few nights ago."

"Why do you provoke him so, Rosalind?"

"I do not provoke him. Not intentionally, anyway. He treats me as if I'm a prisoner."

"Therefore, you simply *must* attempt to escape."

"It's human nature." For a long moment, the two sat in silence, staring at one another as the tension between them thickened. "Whose side are you on?" Rosalind finally asked.

That brought a more cynical smile to his expression. "Must I choose sides now, Rosalind? Has this become a game for you? For if it has, let me warn you. You are playing too deep, dear. You cannot win. Stay at home, be a good girl, and mind your daddy.

You've no business sneaking out of your house to scour taverns such as this. You'll wind up with more trouble than you know what to do with."

Rosalind rankled at his patronizing tone, but said nothing. He didn't know why she'd come to The Salty Dog. He couldn't. The tavern was empty when she'd asked the bartender if he knew a man named Redd Fellowes. Perhaps Lord Pershing thought she was on a lark, seeking a wild adventure in an attempt to provoke her over-protective father. Well, if that was what he thought, she wouldn't disabuse him of the notion. Her mission to find Redd Fellowes was none of his business, anyway.

"You're asking for trouble." His features hardened. The crescent shadows beneath his eyes darkened.

"I'm not afraid," Rosalind said, her voice little more than a whisper.

But, she was. The stillness of Rafe's body frightened her. The raw intensity of his stare filled her with a tingly dread. There was hunger in his stare, and a tension that vibrated beneath the surface of his skin. Yet, he remained perfectly still, as if all his emotions and urges were barely suppressed beneath that cool exterior.

She tossed off her lap blanket and sat beside him. His gaze followed her, but still he didn't move a muscle.

"I have decided to abide by your father's wishes," he said.

Rosalind snapped off her gloves, then reached for his hand.

Instinctively, his fingers formed a tight leather ball

against his thigh. He made a protest deep in his throat, and his entire body tensed.

"I don't believe you." Her ache to feel his flesh against hers was strong. She gathered his right hand in both of hers, and unwound his clenched fist. Slowly, she straightened his fingers, holding his gaze while she slid her hand down his wrist, removing his kid gloves, pulling each finger free. Then, she stroked the back of his hand, measured the pulse pounding in his wrist, felt the heat of his flesh beneath her touch.

"Rosalind, don't." His flashing eyes warned her off.

Turning his hand, she traced the lines in his palm. "You want me, don't you?"

"What I want is of no consequence. You are too young and too innocent for the likes of me."

Her gaze was fixed on his lips. She knew what they felt like against her bare shoulders. She knew what the bristles of his beard felt like when they scraped her neck. "I'm surprised that you would let Father make that decision for you."

"It's my decision, Rosalind."

She sat on the edge of the squab, studying him. After a length, she said, "You told me you were lonely, Rafe. You said so yourself. You said what I needed was a real man, a grown man, not some clumsy boy who thinks the moon is made of green cheese."

His gaze softened. "You've got a fantasy about the sort of man you want, Rosalind. But that's all it is, a fantasy. You'll get over your infatuation with me, and then you'll be glad I didn't seriously pursue you."

"But, the way you kissed me . . . were you simply trifling with me?"

"I was wrong to kiss you that way. I pray to God you'll forgive me some day."

"Forgive you?" A queasiness bubbled up in Rosalind's stomach. "Then, you regret it?"

He closed his eyes for a moment, as if recalling their encounter. When he opened them, there was a coldness in his gaze that chilled her straight through to the marrow in her bones. "It was wrong, I tell you. You and I can never be more than friends. And friends we must be, because we are to see one another at the Toppainsley's dinner party this weekend. Your father has given me strict orders not to court you. And I intend to follow those orders. That is my decision, Rosalind, and it is final. Please do not make it any more difficult than it already is."

She pulled her hand from his, and quickly slipped on her glove. A slap in the face couldn't have made her cheeks sting more violently, or her heart race faster. Unnerved and humiliated, she returned to her seat opposite the viscount's. Blinking hard, she barely managed not to cry. When she thought she could control her voice, she said, "Why did you get in this carriage this morning, then, Rafe? Why didn't you simply ignore me when you saw me on the street?"

"Because you are a woman alone in a place you shouldn't be. I owe it to you *as a friend* to see that you get home safely. I would be remiss in my duties as a gentleman were I to ignore you." He tapped his hat on his head, and reached for the door handle. "I am going to instruct the driver to take you home and nowhere else. Have him stop at the corner near your house, if you must, and sneak in through the root cellar. 'Tis none of my concern how you conduct your subterfuge, but I'll not have it on my conscience that you got yourself in trouble while prowling around taverns. Not while I knew about it, anyway!"

"Don't worry, my lord. You'll not be implicated if I get into trouble. I may be young, but I'm not a tattletale."

His lips tightened. She'd hit a nerve, and she knew it. But he held his tongue and opened the carriage door. He easily stepped to the ground, then turned, and before closing the door, added, "Go back to your daddy, Rosalind. That's where you belong."

The carriage returned to Brighton, and as it tumbled over the rutted road, Rosalind's emotions jolted and shifted like loose luggage on the rooftop rack. By the time she crawled into her bed, she was bewildered to the point of nausea. Her sickness gave her an excuse to hide from Dovie the rest of the day.

But she couldn't escape her feelings, or the realization that she'd made a terrible blunder with Rafe Lawless, Viscount Pershing. Mistaking his kisses for affection had left her vulnerable to his cruelty. She'd been a fool to trust Rafe, a naive greenie who'd let an older, more sophisticated widower toy with her emotions.

She'd best forget all about him. That's what her father wanted her to do anyway.

Pulling the counterpane over her head, Rosalind pictured herself at the Toppainsley's dinner party, chatting gaily with everyone in the room except Rafe, to whom she intended to give the cut direct. The thrill of revenge sliced through her. She hadn't quite figured it all out, but she'd get even with the viscount for what he'd done to her. She'd show him in the end that he couldn't trifle with Rosalind Yardley's affections and walk away from her unscathed.

Lady Dovie tiptoed around Rosalind's room, first picking up the morning gown tossed over a chair, then bending to study the soles of the half-boots strewn on the floor.

With one eye open, Rosalind watched the woman who had taken her mother's place. Or tried to. A top-heavy blonde with a taste for brightly colored frocks covered in bows and ribbons, Lady Dovie Yardley was the antithesis of Rosalind's deceased mother. It was as if Sir Sibbald had chosen a second wife as different from his first as humanly possible. And it was a choice that Rosalind never would understand.

From the beginning, Rosalind's relationship with Dovie had been strained. The last three years, during which Rosalind had endured three London seasons, produced particularly strained communications. Dovie wanted to marry off her stepdaughter so that she would finally have Sir Sibbald's attentions all to herself. At least, that's what Rosalind thought.

And Rosalind couldn't bear the thought of getting married and leaving Sir Sibbald alone, in the clutches of that conniving little canary Dovie. If she married, she might never see her father again. Dovie would shut Rosalind out completely, and poison her father's mind so that his daughter would be a forgotten relative, somewhat distant and vague. Like the memory of Rosalind's mother.

In the far reaches of her mind, Rosalind continued to harbor some dim hope that Sir Sibbald would realize he'd been wrong to marry Dovie, a woman so far beneath the standards set by Rosalind's mother, a woman unfit to *serve* Rosalind's mother.

So, Rosalind had only halfheartedly participated in the marriage markets that took place each spring. On principle, she'd rejected Dovie's advice on everything from dresses to suitors. And she'd rebuffed every gentleman who'd seriously courted her.

She hadn't even kissed a man before she'd met Lord Pershing. Not *really*. She'd allowed a few men to bestow a peck on her cheek, and once, she'd even allowed a handsome gent to draw her into his arms and kiss her passionately on the lips. But she'd never really been kissed before Rafe happened into her life. Now that she had, she understood what all the ruckus was about. No wonder the mamas at the Marriage Mart were so nervous when their babies waltzed behind a row of potted palms and became invisible for five minutes. Much could happen in five minutes.

The memory of Rafe's lips pressed hard against hers and the ragged sound of his breathing against her neck, made her nerve endings dance. With one arm flung across her eyes, she fought the heat pooling in her lower body. She should hate Lord Pershing for the way he'd treated her this morning. He spoke to her as if she were a baby! Yet there was something in his pained expression that painted a lie on his cruel words. Or, was she simply fooling herself?

Miserable, Rosalind peeked out from beneath her arm. Dovie was studiously examining the hem of a linen rail that Rosalind had tossed over her tole screen. Resentment and defiance swirled in Rosalind's stomach as her stepmother fingered the delicate lace edging. Dovie was a nuisance. Her opinions were fluff, and her advice was useless. And her enthusiastic endorsement of Sir Sibbald's rejection of Lord Pershing simply made the viscount more attractive.

But, with a heavy sigh, Rosalind reminded herself that Pershing was a cad. She'd spent the morning resolving to ignore him at the Toppainsley's party. She intended to stick to her plan. Just because she'd be pleasing Dovie into the bargain was no reason to change her mind.

Dovie abruptly turned. "Are you awake, dear?"

"I am now." Rosalind struggled to her elbows.

"Where have you been?"

Anger, rather than nervousness, shot through Rosalind's veins. "I've been here, in bed. Didn't my abigail tell you? I've had a sick stomach all morning."

"It's two in the afternoon, dear. If you're that sick, perhaps I should send a porter to fetch the doctor."

Rosalind fell back on a pile of bolsters, exasperated. "I don't need a doctor. I'm better now."

Dovie crossed the room and stood beside her bed. "You weren't poisoned, too, were you?"

"No." Rosalind tucked the counterpane beneath

her arms and closed her eyes. "But it was a long night, Dovie, and I'm tired."

"Yes, I suppose you are. It must be awfully tiring on you, sneaking in and out of this house the way you do."

Thanking the lord that her eyes were shut, Rosalind feigned an expression of utter unconcern. "What on earth are you babbling about, Dovie?"

"I'm not a fool, Rosie."

"You are if you think I've left this bed since I crawled into it last night."

After a beat, during which Rosalind heard Dovie's sharp intake of breath, the older woman said quietly, "I've had quite enough of your insolence, Rosalind. For years, I've ignored your barbs and your slights because I felt sorry for you. I was sorry that you lost your dear mother. And I was even sorry that you lost a bit of your father, as well."

"You've no idea how I feel," Rosalind whispered.

"I don't pretend to. But your anger has little to do with me personally. You hated me before I set foot in this house. You would have hated anyone who tried to take your mother's place."

Rosalind's eyes flung open, and she stared at Dovie. "Then why did you come here?"

"Because I love your father. It's as simple as that. And I suppose I foolishly thought that with time, you'd grow accustomed to me. I didn't try to take your mother's place, Rosie. I knew I couldn't. I'm nothing like her, and I never will be. But your father loves me for what I am, and if that's good enough for him, you should try to accept me. For your father's sake, if not for your own."

"Father made a mistake." Rosalind's voice trembled. "We would have been fine, just the two of us. I could have taken care of him."

"Do you think that's what your mother would have wanted, dear? For the two of you to be alone?"

Stung, Rosalind turned her face into the pillows. Tears streamed down her cheeks, and her breath came in jagged gasps. "We were a family, the three of us. You've taken Father from me—"

Dovie's voice was surprisingly gentle. "Your father loves you more than anyone in the world. I couldn't take him from you if I tried, Rosalind."

"He isn't like he was before." Rosalind hiccoughed, struggling for the words in which to frame her emotions. "He's different, he's changed."

"Yes, I suppose he has changed." Dovie perched herself on the edge of the bed. She laid her hand on Rosalind's shoulder, but she didn't try to smother her in an embrace, and for that, Rosalind was grateful. For once, Rosalind appreciated Dovie's lack of pretense. The woman's wardrobe might have been full of frippery, but her emotions were amazingly unadorned.

"You've much to learn," Dovie continued. "Life is full of change. Sometimes the change is good, sometimes it's not. But, your character is measured by how you react to that change, how you adapt to it. Cherishing your memories is good and wise, but clinging to the past is dangerous. You want so badly to be grown up, Rosalind. Well, to start, you must accept that your life was unalterably changed when your mother died. So was your father's. Neither of you can go back, but you still have each other. And the future. I don't mean to be rude, dear, but you're being a baby."

Rosalind's heart ached. She had a fleeting, instinctive urge to throw herself into Dovie's arms and sob for forgiveness, but pride and confusion restrained her. Dovie's criticism cut her deeply, and she didn't know whether her stepmother's embrace would provide sanctuary or recrimination. Shielding herself with anger, she squeezed her eyes shut again, and said, "Please go away."

Dovie stood. "Anger will stunt your growth quicker than Turkish coffee, dear."

Unable to speak, Rosalind waved her stepmother away.

At the door, the woman paused. "I don't know where you went this morning, but I will be keeping a closer watch over you, Rosalind. Your father would be devastated if something happened to you. And I do not intend to stand idly by and watch you break his heart. Your mother's death was hard enough on him as it was. He couldn't live with the thought of your being hurt."

The door clicked shut behind her, and the room was suddenly engulfed by silence. Rosalind turned on her stomach and cried until her ribs ached. Dovie's observations were like sharp knives jabbing at her conscience. At that moment, she hated the woman more than she ever had.

What was worse, she hated herself, too.

* * *

Jemmy Pratt rolled another oaken cask through the cellar door. "That's the last one, m'lord. Think I'll call it a night."

Standing at the long trestle table that served as a tasting board, Lord Pershing nodded. A beat passed before he realized someone had spoken. Suddenly, he heard what had been said. When he looked at the man, in his striped sailor's shirt and loose-fitting trousers, he smiled apologetically.

"Sorry, m'lord. Didn't mean to interrupt. How's the wine?"

Rafe swallowed. "Not as good as last year's. Have a taste, Pratt."

Tom Wickham descended the stone steps which led from the main house to the cellar. "Drinking up our inventory are you?"

"It's important to know what we're selling, Tom. Especially when we're demanding such a premium price for this white Bordeaux. Here, have a glass." Rafe poured two glasses, one for Pratt, the other for Tom.

Throwing back his head, Pratt inhaled the straw-colored liquid in one long gulp.

Tom carefully swirled, sniffed and sipped, drawing the wine through his teeth on a deep breath. "Tastes like a meadow, if you ask me," he said, at length.

Chuckling, Rafe said, "It's a bit on the grassy side, I'll agree."

Pratt shot both men a quizzical look. "Tastes like white wine to me. I'll allow it's a mite tart—"

"Green apples," murmured Tom, his eyes closed.

Rafe took another sip. "With a flinty undertone."

Pratt set his empty glass on the tasting table. "Don't know what the hell you two are gabbin' about. I'll stick with me beer and me apple-jack." He touched the brim of his sailor's cap and turned to leave.

"Before you go, Pratt, I've got a delivery for you to make." Rafe pointed to a towering column of small wooden crates stacked against the wall. "I want you to deliver a case of that red Bordeaux to Lord Toppainsley's town house in Brighton."

Tom nearly choked on his mouthful of wine. "Lord Toppainsley? Are you certain, Rafe? He's a close friend of Sir Sibbald, for God's sake. I doubt seriously if—"

"We'll find out, won't we? I don't intend to put my calling card on the wine, Tom. Jemmy, see that the wine is left in the alley behind Toppainsley's kitchen. Make certain that no one sees you, do you understand?"

"I'm not sure I do, m'lord. You want to send some of yer finest goods to this Lord Toppainsley as a gift, but ye don't want him to know who's sendin' it?"

"That's it." Rafe winked at Tom. "It's an experiment. Trust me."

"Apparently I do," replied Tom, draining his wineglass. "Otherwise, I would have married an heiress long ago."

Rafe started to reply, but, realizing Jemmy Pratt remained in the doorway, staring at him, said, "Any questions, Pratt? Here, this case will do." He put down his glass, strode to the stack of wine cases, and hefted the top one into Jemmy's arms.

Pratt staggered backward. "Anything else, m'lord?"

"That will be all." Rafe watched the man disappear through the cellar door. Returning to the tasting table, he poured more wine into his and Tom's glasses. "I told you, I have a suspicion about Lord Toppainsley, and I believe this little donation will either confirm it or refute it."

"Do you seriously think he's in the market for some contraband liquor? Or some fine French wine?"

"Is there any other explanation for his sudden interest in us? We're not exactly the pink of the ton, Tom. In fact, we're two of the most unsociable gents around."

Tom bristled. "We're respectable. I met Lord Toppainsley in a respectable enough establishment. He took a liking to me."

"No offense, but his interest in me seemed keener than his affection for you."

"Why shouldn't it be? You have a title, by God!"

"But very little money, at least as far as the general public is concerned. A smuggler can't very well advertise his wealth, can he? To the casual onlooker, I'm an eccentric widower living in a crumbling old house that is clinging by a single vine to a cliff overlooking the sea. I keep to myself. I frequent The Salty Dog and take my meals alone. Since Annette died, I have not accepted a solitary invitation to a country house party, a dance or a dinner party."

"Until recently, that is."

Rafe's fingers coiled around the base of his wine-glass. He'd done a lot of things recently that he thought he'd never do again. Like accepting invitations to social events. And wishing he weren't sleeping alone in a big, cold bed every night.

The chill seeping up from the stone floor invaded his bones. "Perhaps I should socialize more, Tom."

"I can't believe what I'm hearing."

"Don't you ever get tired of being alone? Don't you ever yearn for a woman to sleep with—a warm, loving woman who will wait up for you at night just to listen to the troubles of your day? A woman who will bear your children and share your life and make a home out of this tottering old house?"

Tom thrust his hands through his unruly curls. "We're not talking about me, are we? Well, if you're itching for a woman, Rafe, go to town and get one. They can be had, dear, for less than the price of a bottle of your precious Bordeaux. For a night, a sen-night, or once a week until your talleywacker falls off. You can even choose one with the color of hair you fancy. If you go to the right establishment, you can even choose from a wide assortment of figure shapes and degrees of adventurousness."

Rafe forced a smile. Tom couldn't possibly know how futile his attempts at humor were. "I'm afraid I can't do that."

"Why not? Don't tell me the starch has gone out of your sails."

"Nothing like that." *In fact, his problem was quite to the contrary.* Rafe shifted his weight, bitterly unhappy about the heaviness weighting his loins. "No, I'm simply not in the proper frame of mind for that sort of bed sport, Tom. It's not mere sex I'm looking for—"

Tom sighed. "Something's happened to you, Rafe. In a matter of days, too. It's as if that Yardley chit had cast some sort of spell over you. Or a wet blanket, I don't know which."

"It has nothing to do with her," Rafe growled.

"I should hope not." Eying him oddly, Tom added, "By the way, what happened after I left you in the alley at The Salty Dog? Did you find out why the esteemed Miss Yardley was there?"

"No. She hopped in her carriage and was gone before I could speak with her."

" 'Tis a mystery. Do you think her father—"

"Her father has asked me to stay away from her, and I've agreed."

"Good!" Tom lowered his wineglass with a clatter. "We've got enough problems right now without having Sir Sibbald breathing down our necks."

Rafe cleared his throat. "I have no intentions of ever touching Rosalind Yardley again. You needn't worry on that score."

"I should never have allowed you to waltz with her. I should have done the deed myself, and spun the little bit of baggage right out the window! Sorry, old man, I won't let her latch onto you like that again, I swear it."

"Come on, Tom, we've got business to conduct. And if I'm going to a dinner party, I suppose I need to polish my slippers, don't I?"

Tom chuckled. "It's not too late to cancel."

"I have no intention of canceling. We are attending this dinner party purely for business reasons." As the two men headed toward the staircase leading up to the house, Rafe linked his arm through Tom's. "On second thought, old man, do you know the name of one of those establishments you were referring to? Where a man can, er, have a lady . . . for the evening?"

"Mrs. Simca's on Feathergale Lane. Here's the address." Tom pulled a small card from his vest pocket. "Tell Mrs. Simca you're a friend of mine. She'll take care of you."

Rafe winced. He'd sought comfort in the arms of strangers before, and he'd never had a twinge of guilt. Why did it seem so objectionable now? Why, suddenly, did he feel so guilty and dirty for wanting sex with a willing woman?

Because what he truly wanted was the comfort of Miss Rosalind Yardley's arms—something he couldn't have. *Something he didn't want.* At least, that's what he told himself as he took Mrs. Simca's calling card from Tom's fingers.

Eight

Though Rafe had never heard of Feathergale Lane, he had little trouble locating Mrs. Simca's house. The short, dead-end street was discreetly wedged between a block of cobblers' shops and mantua makers. As Tom Wickham had predicted, a gas lantern illuminated the gleaming gold numbers above the front door.

Mrs. Simca's was the sort of place one might pass a hundred times and never notice. But, it was an amazingly easy address to find if a man was looking for it.

Standing on the front steps, Rafe thought the pale yellow brick establishment seemed incongruously neat and pretty, as respectable looking a place as any dowager could imagine. But, the moment he grasped the heavy brass knocker, a raw impulse jolted through him. His pulse quickened as the sound of masculine footsteps approached the door. When it opened, he didn't even bother to smile at the African gentleman who greeted him.

"Good evening. What might I do for you?" Clad

in a gold brocade jacket, knee breeches, and shiny patent leather slippers, the butler was the picture of elegance. His smile revealed rows of perfect white teeth, and his gaze held a sort of gentle keenness.

"I've come to see Mrs. Simca."

"Is she expecting you?"

Rafe produced an engraved calling card which the butler accepted in his white glove. "Tom Wickham referred me to her."

The black gentleman bowed, straightened, then ushered Rafe into the house. "Follow me."

Up the staircase and down a short hallway was a drawing room. Devouring the entire length of the house, the room was sectioned off into cozy little alcoves, or intimate sitting areas, so that even when filled with people, couples could establish a degree of privacy among themselves. Glancing about the candle-lit parlor, Rafe saw at least a half-dozen men in seemingly earnest conversation with scantily dressed women. For a fleeting instant, he wondered what on earth they could be talking about.

Then, a sense of sadness overwhelmed him as he realized the men and women here were probably discussing the most urbane of subjects—politics, perhaps, the latest news regarding the war, or a recent marriage announcement. After all, wasn't companionship and warmth what men wanted from women more than anything? Even men who frequented brothels wanted more than sex. The most rapacious scoundrel, at the bottom of his heart, just wanted someone to love him and listen to him and care what he thought.

But if spiritual succor was unavailable, a man still wanted physical satisfaction.

The butler gestured toward a crimson banquette, tucked snugly in a shadowy corner. "Make yourself comfortable, Mister—"

"Thank you." Rafe had gained admittance to Mrs. Simca's with the mention of Tom Wickham's name; he saw no reason to reveal his own identity.

Sinking into the soft red velvet, he mentally upbraided himself. The soft murmur of conversation was punctuated with the occasional tinkle of female laughter. The sounds of flirtation annoyed him. He didn't come to Mrs. Simca's to talk. He'd come because of his sudden burning desire for a woman, any woman. He'd come to Mrs. Simca's because ridding himself of his sexual need would make him less vulnerable to the charms and wiles of Miss Rosalind Yardley. At least, that was his theory.

"Bon soir." A middle-aged red-headed woman stood before him with a bottle of champagne in one hand, and two crystal flutes laced between the fingers of her other. An almost transparent peignoir revealed an ample but shapely figure, and when she leaned forward, displaying the bottle to Rafe, a bountiful amount of bosom spilled forth.

Rafe smiled politely. "Thank you, but I have no taste for champagne this evening."

The woman's smile was wistful, but her eyes were understanding. Straightening, she said, "Would you care for something else?"

"I haven't decided yet."

She moved away on high-heeled slippers, and the

sight of her derriere, as ample as her bosom and as lush as the velvet sofa he'd sunk into, stirred Rafe's hunger.

Moments later, a blond woman in her late twenties materialized bearing two tall glasses filled with a frothy liquid and studded with fruit. With her willowy figure and swan-like neck, she could have posed for a French fashion plate. Instead of the filmy boudoir attire worn by many of Mrs. Simca's girls, she modeled an elegant cream colored evening gown, low-cut in the current fashion, but tasteful enough to grace the most exclusive salon in Mayfair.

Her smile, demure but full of promise, revealed perfect white teeth. Her gaze, direct, but not too brazen, added fuel to Rafe's arousal. Her voice, sultry but not provocative, sounded like the deep-throated purr of a fully mature, supremely spoiled house cat. The overall effect was of a tightly repressed aristocrat who might become a tigress in the bedchamber.

"Punch, my lord?"

Rafe shook his head. His throat constricted and when he answered the woman, his voice sound a bit more scratchy than he would have preferred. "Thank you, but I'm not in the mood for a syrupy drink this evening."

"Tell me what you would like, my lord, and I'll see to it that you're taken care of. Mrs. Simca wouldn't want a man to leave here with his thirst unslaked."

The cynicism in the woman's gaze caused Rafe's arousal to flag. "I'm not certain what I want."

The blond woman lifted her chin a notch, made her lips a compact line, and turned on her heel.

Watching her, Rafe felt inexplicably embarrassed. For her and for himself. In this strange environment, refusing to take a woman was considered an insult to her. Yet, Rafe couldn't have made love to that woman if a pistol had been held to his head and his life depended upon it.

Suddenly weary, he extracted a small silver snuffbox from his pocket and took a fortifying sniff. The sting of the powder cleared his head. Having concluded he should leave, Rafe pushed off the banquette with every intention of doing so. But, when he stood, he was face-to-face with another woman, this one holding a single shot glass and a bottle of whiskey.

"Hello." Her smile faltered as her gaze searched his face.

Had Rafe not been afraid of the answer, he would have asked the young woman her age. Instead, he took the bottle and glass from her, poured himself a neat drink and invited her to sit beside him. When they were side by side on the velvet banquette, he threw back his head and drained the glass.

Suppressing a shudder, he asked, "What's your name?"

"The other girls call me Baby." She had thick, lustrous black hair and a full-cheeked, heart-shaped face. Her breasts were small but sat up high and her wrists were as thin and delicate as a china doll's. He allowed her to lead him down the hallway and up the stairs, into a small room fitted out with bed, washstand, and armoire. Once inside, she turned to face him, both demure and seductive, before she sat down on the bed.

"Baby," he repeated hoarsely. His mouth was cottony and his throat burned. "How long have you been here?"

Her hands sat primly in her lap; her ankles were glued together. "I'm brand new. This is my first night as a matter of fact."

"First night?" As he poured himself a shot and sat down beside her, the implications of that remark slowly sank in on Rafe. "But, before tonight—"

Her eyes widened.

"Before tonight, you were with—"

She continued to stare at him, her pastel eyes round in the shadows.

"You don't mean to say . . ." Unnerved, he took one of her hands in his. He felt a tremor race through her body when he touched her. Her gaze flickered, but returned to his, and there was a tentativeness in her pulse as he ran his fingertips along the sensitive underside of her wrist. "You're not suggesting that you're a virgin, are you?"

Her chin wobbled. "Yes," she whispered. "If you make love to me tonight, you will be the first."

Rafe's heart squeezed like a fist, and he thought for a moment that he might lose consciousness. A wave of desire swept over him, followed by the reverse tug of a guilty ebb tide. The thought of taking this young girl's virginity held infinite erotic appeal, and yet the moral responsibility of robbing a girl of her maidenhead boggled his mind.

Swallowing hard, he shook his head. "No."

She leaned forward, pressing both her hands into his larger ones. "Please, Mister—"

"Rafe."

"Please, Rafe. If you don't, someone else will. Mrs. Simca will not allow me to stay here unless I can support myself. I must learn how to pleasure a man, and if you don't teach me, I might wind up with some unpleasant ogre who takes pleasure from being cruel."

"And how do you know I won't be cruel to you?"

"Because I can see it in your eyes. You're a kind man, and you will love me properly. Please, Rafe. Make love to me."

"I can't." He withdrew his hands, and pinched the bridge of his nose. "I cannot do it."

Her voice was a mere breath against his neck. "Why? Is there something wrong, Rafe?"

"No."

She pressed her firm little breasts against his shoulder. "I want you to be the first, Rafe. I've chosen you. Please."

The ache of his desire was powerful. Rafe closed his eyes, willing himself to resist the young woman's entreaty. He'd not bedded a virgin since he was one himself, and he harbored no fantasies about deflowering an innocent. What was more, he had no fetish for untrained greenies lacking the maturity to make wise decisions, and the notion of taking advantage of a woman did not excite him. In a heartbeat, his need wilted.

"I'm sorry," he managed. He reached into his pocket and extracted a wad of paper currency. "I can't. I mean, I don't want to."

Her expression was full of disbelief. "What's the matter? Got a war wound or something?"

"No."

"Am I not attractive enough for you?"

"It isn't you."

"Do you prefer another woman?"

"Yes." Of course, he preferred another woman. "No." But, that other woman wasn't here.

"I don't understand." Baby's forehead creased, and her voice took on a distinctly grown-up tenor. "You're willing to pay, but you don't want me to lay down with you? Are you some sort of deviant?"

"No." He took a step backward. "I just want to go. I made a mistake. I'm sorry if I've inconvenienced you, or troubled you in any way. Here, the money's yours."

He was startled at how quickly the money changed hands. When Baby had counted the bills, carefully folded them, and tucked them beneath the neckline of her gown, she gave him a long, searching look. "Don't go, anyhow. Not just yet. If you do, Mrs. Simca will have me back in the parlor quicker than you can say jack flash." She turned and pulled a silken bell cord beside her wash stand. "Care for a cup of tea?"

"Won't Mrs. Simca be just as annoyed to learn you're taking tea with me in your room, instead of—"

"Some men like to talk." Baby shrugged. "Some men would rather talk than—"

"Ridiculous! I didn't come here to talk." Rafe flushed with embarrassment, feeling somehow as if his bluff had been called. Was his confusion too obvious? Was he so transparent that even a virgin could recognize his unhappiness? Had he sunk so low that the sympathy of a prostitute named Baby was now welcome?

"Well, you didn't come here for sex, that's readily apparent. Don't talk if you'd rather not, but I'm a good listener, and there's no one I could tell who would care a fig, so your secrets are safer with me than if they were locked in a vault in the Bank of England."

Rafe pivoted, and placed his hand on the doorknob. But he hesitated to leave. His body had ceased its throbbing, but his heart remained heavy with regret and indecision. Releasing the brass knob, he slowly turned and faced the prostitute.

"If it makes you feel any better," she said, "my name is Adelaide, not Baby, and I'm twenty-seven years old, not seventeen."

"You're not a virgin, then?"

Her smile was surprisingly full of warmth. "Hardly."

After a beat, during which Rafe quickly reassessed the previous half hour, he laughed heartily. The relief that spread through his body was liberating. Perhaps the joke was on him, but there was something about Adelaide he found refreshing.

A servant knocked on the door, and discreetly delivered a small tray laden with a pot of tea, two cups, and a plate of sweet biscuits.

Adelaide and Rafe sat on the edge of the bed, sipping tea.

"I had you going there for a little while, didn't I?"

She popped a biscuit in her mouth and grinned while she ate.

"You're quite an actress."

"Not really. I was a virgin once, believe it or not."

"Tell me, Adelaide. What is the appeal of pretending to be one again?"

"Some think that making love is a purely physical act." She tapped the side of her head. "But, it's all in here, really." Then, she touched her breastbone. "And in here. We all want to be loved, don't we? And being the strange, complicated creatures that we are, we often look to our bed mates to satisfy our deepest cravings, to fill the emptiness we feel in our souls."

"Are you suggesting that a man's sexual impulses, more particularly, his proclivities, reflect his attempts to resolve his own inadequacies?"

"Men who were ignored by their mothers often want to make love to an older woman. Men who were bullied by their mothers sometimes seek revenge on the opposite sex." Adelaide wrinkled her nose.

"And men who come here with the fantasy of making love to a virgin?"

She arched her brows. Over the rim of her teacup, she said, "You tell me, Rafe. What did you hope to find here?"

He put down his teacup, and stood beside the bed. "I don't know, Adelaide. But, I didn't expect to find a philosopher. I don't mean to sound trite, but what are you doing in a place like this? You're much too clever to spend the rest of your life making your living on your back."

Sadness glimmered in her eyes. "Like I said, Rafe,

we're all trying to make up for our inadequacies. Shall I walk you to the door?"

He shook his head. "No." Then, before she could stand, he leaned down and kissed the top of her head. She lifted her chin and looked up. The child-like expression of Baby had returned, uncloaked by the tough wisdom of Adelaide's cynical gaze. "Take care of yourself."

When he left Mrs. Simca's, Rafe was miserable, convinced that his discomfort had little to do with his physical state and more to do with the spiritual vacuum he'd been living in since his wife Annette had died.

Yet, his encounter with Adelaide had sobered him to the wiles of Miss Rosalind Yardley. Rosalind's innocence held an erotic appeal, yes. But, intrigue swirled around her. Her father could arrest him, recommend him for prosecution, and see him hung. Considering the recent attempt on his life, and the sudden difficulty he was having with his customers, Rafe wasn't entirely certain Sir Sibbald wasn't already on his trail.

And for all Rosalind's wide-eyed protests of innocence, and chin-trembling confessions of neediness, he couldn't—and shouldn't—trust her. If he hadn't learned from Annette that women were unpredictable creatures, he'd certainly learned from Adelaide that they were masters of disguise. They started out wanting one thing, then wound up wanting something else. Sometimes, they lied about what they wanted; sometimes they simply didn't know their own needs.

Whoever Rosalind Yardley was, Rafe Lawless intended to keep his distance from her. Whatever she wanted, she'd have to find it elsewhere.

Despite the rocky pitch of the viscount's carriage as it rumbled toward Brighton, Tom Wickham managed to hold a pinch of snuff to his nostrils and inhale smartly. After a full-body shudder, he offered the box to his companion and grinned.

Rafe did not grin back. "It's going to be a difficult landing tonight." He glanced through the window at the passing blackness. It was a star-studded night, but the chill in the air was formidable. "At least we won't be needing to light torches to guide the dinghies to shore. We've drawn far too much attention to ourselves of late. Our luck is bound to run out one of these nights."

"Care for a pinch of my snuff, old man? Might make you feel better."

"No thanks." Rafe favored his own blend. However, when his hand instinctively reached into his pocket, he found his snuff box missing. He muttered a colorful oath. "I must have lost my snuff box at Mrs. Simca's."

Despite Rafe's foul mood, Tom smiled. "You haven't told me what happened there. Did you enjoy yourself?"

"It was a bloody disaster, Tom. How the hell do you tolerate the place?"

With a shrug, Tom snapped his snuff box shut. "I quite fancy the place. Did you meet Baby?"

"Indeed."

After a length, Tom said, "What did you think?"

"It saddened me."

"It *saddened* you?" Tom scratched his head. "I have to admit, Rafe, I don't understand you of late."

"I'm not certain I understand myself."

"Perhaps you should see a doctor."

"There is nothing wrong with me physically," Rafe growled, tired of that particular line of inquiry. He slammed one fist into his open palm. "Tom, have you given any thought to your future?"

The abrupt change of conversational direction clearly stunned Tom. "My future?"

"Our future."

"Together?"

"Damme, man! Don't vex me!" Rafe's patience was near the breaking point. "I haven't been this miserable since Annette became so ill. The helplessness of watching her suffer, of knowing that I could do nothing to ease her pain, was unbearable. What I'm feeling now is nearly that bad, Tom."

"You've lost me, Rafe."

"I'm talking about the rest of our lives." Rafe leaned forward, pounding the air with his fist as if he were trying to hammer some understanding into Tom's head. "We've spent the last five years living underground, as it were, hiding our true activities. I'm beginning to feel like a trapped rat, and I don't like it."

"I thought you enjoyed the excitement of it. I thought you believed in the politics of it. What about all those impassioned speeches you made about the ignorant asses who are running our government, imposing taxes on foreign goods when to do so merely injures our own economy and impoverishes our people?"

"I suppose if I want to change government, I should run for a seat in the House, shouldn't I? Or put my pen to paper and write radical essays."

"Yes, well, say hello to Mr. Hunt while you're rotting in prison," quipped Tom, referring to the famous reform party leader who had so offended Prinny.

"Mr. Hunt probably sleeps more soundly at night than I."

"You'd sleep better if you had a woman. That's what I sent you to Mrs. Simca's for."

"A man goes to Mrs. Simca's for sex, not love. Any decent woman wouldn't waste her time on a smuggler, Tom. As it is now, I have nothing to offer a woman. I'm always looking over my shoulder, always suspicious of everyone. What sort of life is that?"

"Has this something to do with Sir Sibbald Yardley and the Toppainsleys?"

Rafe sighed, pushed back against the seat cushions and folded his arms across his chest. "I'm afraid it has more to do with Miss Rosalind Yardley."

It was Tom's turn to sigh with exasperation. "Haven't we discussed this, Rafe? She's out of boundaries for you. You can't afford to trifle with that woman. Especially now when there's trouble brewing with our customers and we don't know why."

"But, that's my point, Tom." Rafe turned and stared out the window, his gaze finding some invisible point of starlight that remained fixed even as the landscape slid by. "I'm tired of feeling like an outcast. I'm tired of mourning the life I had with Annette. I loved her, but she's gone. And I'm tired of waiting for my life to begin again.''

"You're not thinking of quitting, are you?"

Rafe didn't answer, but stared into his friend's wide blinking eyes, wondering what their futures would be like if they embarked on a legal enterprise, something they could be proud of, something they could feel good about.

"Just don't make the same mistake twice," Tom said, taking another pinch of snuff.

Ordinarily, such an irreverent reference to Rafe's deceased wife would have offended him. But, Tom was right. Rafe had made a mistake when he married a girl whose father looked down on him. When Annette recovered from her infatuation, when her need to shock her parents and rebel against her father had subsided, she spent the rest of her marriage suffering in quiet discontent. Rafe had often wondered if boredom and regret hadn't killed her, rather than the malignancy that the surgeons said had consumed her bones.

Don't make the same mistake twice.

The words lodged in Rafe's brain like an anchor in silt. They added an edge to his already black mood, an edge that couldn't be dulled by a snort of powdered tobacco. Rafe watched as his friend's expression melted to one of tranquility. He wished his melancholy could be banished by drink or medicine. He'd even tried to vanquish his depression with the oldest vice of all, but that had left him more dissatisfied with himself than before.

What he needed was a change, a sea-change that

would alter his course and set him in the right direction. But, he was like a rudderless boat, drifting in the ocean. One tall wave could crush him. One lucky wisp of wind could save his soul.

The carriage slowed, then jerked to a halt in front of Lord Toppainsley's town house. His mood having improved not one iota, Rafe emerged from the equipage with a curse on his lips.

"Don't know why I accepted this invitation."

Tom stood beside him on the slick, cobbled stones, his breath frosting the air as he gave a huff of friendly derision. "Something about Toppainsley's being a potential customer, I think."

"Thank you for reminding me." Rafe's cloak swirled around him as he stalked toward the house.

Tom fell into step behind him, and the carriage rattled half-way down the block to await their return. From inside the house wafted the angelic sounds of a harp accompanied by the percussive sounds of laughter. Tom and Rafe were most certainly the latest arrivals to the dinner party, since they drove from Rye, and the other guests traveled no more than a few city blocks to get to the Toppainsley's.

A thick row of shrubs braced by wrought iron fencing bordered the apron shaped yard. Lanterns bracketing the front door threw pools of shifting light across the quarry stone path. An unusually strong gust of wind rustled the bushes and deepened the chill in Rafe's bones. He cursed again, this time at the weather, as he thought of the long night that awaited him, unloading a fresh shipment of wine from France, transporting it to his cellar, conducting an inspection of the casks, and preparing the goods to be resold.

"What did you say?" Tom asked, dogging his heels.

"I said—" Rafe halted, falling silent.

A click—the rasp of metal against metal—pricked his ears.

In a split second, he reacted by instinct, pivoting on his heel and throwing his body at Tom's.

"Oomph!" The men fell to the ground and rolled.

The crack of a pistol split the air, shattering a rock in the path where Rafe and Tom had just stood. Then, a movement rustled in the greenery that hugged the house, and a second later, a horse's hooves pounded down the alleyway, fading into the distance as Tom's labored breathing filled Rafe's ears.

"For God's sake, get off me!"

Rafe realized he had covered Tom's body with his own. Locked in an intimate embrace with his best friend, he couldn't suppress a bitter chuckle. Rolling to his knees, he quickly rose to his full height and offered Tom a hand.

"Really, dear." Tom's voice quavered as he made a show of brushing the knees of his satin breeches. "I am starting to worry about you. First, you can't find a woman at Mrs. Simca's who interests you. Then, you tell me you're thinking about hanging up the smuggling business. And, finally, as if that weren't enough, you tackle me as if *I* were the object of your ardent fascination!"

"If I hadn't jumped on you, you'd very likely have

a bullet in your forehead right now." Rafe brushed off his own clothes, then slapped Tom on the back.

"That's no excuse." Despite his flippant tone, Tom heaved a sigh of relief.

A shiver wracked Tom's shoulders as the men hurriedly walked up the path to the front door. Rafe's own fear had passed; whoever shot at them was no longer in the vicinity. Realizing he'd missed his target, the villain fled, like the coward he was.

Footsteps sounded on the other side of the door, even before Rafe had lifted the brass knocker. "Are you alright?" he asked Tom.

"Quite. And you?"

"We don't have to stay."

Tom gave him a challenging look. "Shall we leave?"

"And look like cowards?" Rafe grinned back.

"Were you serious when you said you wanted out of the smuggling business?"

Rafe wasn't certain of much anymore. But, he knew one thing. "I won't be driven from it, Tom. I won't let someone else decide my fate. Someone is trying to destroy me, and I'm going to find out who, and why, if it's the last thing I do."

The door opened to the sight of a fretful butler scanning the street beyond them. "I thought I heard gunfire."

Rafe and Tom exchanged quizzical looks.

Stepping across the threshold, Rafe said, "Didn't hear a thing, did you, old man?"

Tom tossed his cloak to the butler. "No, dear, not a thing."

Nine

Moments later, the men were ushered into the Toppainsley's parlor, a richly textured room drenched in Axminster carpets, Dutch portraits, and heavy, Jacobean furniture. An occasional contemporary piece, gilded in ormolu or topped with marble, blended with artifacts passed down through generations of Toppainsleys. A surprisingly small and free-standing suit of armor guarded one corner of the room, while a pair of crossed swords pinned the family coat of arms to the wall. The effect was that of a museum dedicated to the veneration of a single line of aristocracy.

Sitting catty-corner to the fireplace and the magnificent carved mantelpiece, Lady Toppainsley faintly waggled her fingers in greeting. Sir Sibbald and Lady Dovie, standing on either side of Lady Toppainsley's tapestried throne, stared and murmured, "Hello." Lord Toppainsley strode across the room and welcomed his guests with firm handshakes and hearty hale-fellows. While in the center of the room, sitting on a low stool with her fingers poised at the strings of a huge gilded harp, was Miss Rosalind Yardley, who merely nodded in Rafe's direction, then looked away and began playing a sort of celestial dirge.

Pinching the bridge of his nose, Rafe dared to shoot a glance at Tom whose features were contorted in an effort not to laugh. The Toppainsleys' costumes, right down to the powdered wigs and fake beauty marks, would have been over the top in the Sun King's Versailles. The feigned expressions of normalcy on the Yardleys' faces were comical. Rosalind's now random plucking at the harp was injurious to the ears. The entire scene looked like bad opera.

"The only thing missing is the orange vendor," Tom whispered in Rafe's ear.

Rafe barely managed to school his lips into a vanilla smile. "Good evening, my lord." He released Lord Toppainsley's hand and walked across the room to greet the Lady Toppainsley and the Yardleys. Having said his hellos, he offered an abbreviated bow to Rosalind. She returned his greeting with a tight smile and a blush.

Dinner was uneventful, with Rosalind seated at the far end of the table and on the same side as Rafe so that he couldn't even see her as he ate. Sir Sibbald was doing everything humanly possible to prevent Rafe from speaking to his favored child—so why had Rafe even been invited to this strained, affected dinner party?

After the eight-course meal was finished, the men retired to the library to take snuff, drink port, and discuss topics unsuitable for feminine ears. The women sequestered themselves in the parlor, presumably to talk about needlework or exchange the latest *on dits*.

Lord Toppainsley and Sir Sibbald stood beside the fireplace warming their backsides while Rafe and Tom settled into wingback chairs. After a few minutes talk of horseflesh and the war on the Russian front, the men fell silent.

Tension crackled in the air like the dry firewood burning in the hearth. With a wink at Tom, Rafe settled deeper into his chair and drank his port as if he were the most contented man in the world. "Excellent vintage," he said, holding his glass to the light.

Lord Toppainsley nodded. " 'Tis hard to get good port nowadays."

"I presume you had this in your cellar before the war," Sir Sibbald said with an air of discomfort.

Toppainsley chuckled. "You don't think I smuggled it in, do you? Drink up, Sibbald, old man, my liquors and wines were purchased from legal purveyors before the import tax made it impossible to bring these commodities from the Continent."

Rafe exchanged a knowing look with Toppainsley. The man was feeling him out, he was sure of it, but he'd best tread lightly. "What's worse, it's nearly impossible to find a bottle of good Bordeaux these days."

Tom stirred. "Ah, I do love a good Bordeaux. With a rack of mutton, I think."

"Quite right." Sir Sibbald smacked his lips. "I wouldn't turn down a meal like that. Not if I knew the wine was brought into this country legally.

Damme, but the French do know how to make red wine, don't they?"

"Would you like to taste a little Bordeaux?" Lord Toppainsley pulled a bell cord beside the fireplace. To Sir Sibbald, whose expression had instantly altered to one of astonishment, he said, "Purchased before the war, of course. I think I have a few good bottles left."

When the butler appeared at the double doors of the study, Lord Toppainsley crossed the room and had a few words *sotto voce* with the man. "I asked him to decant it," he explained, returning to the fireplace.

The butler returned shortly, with a crystal decanter and four wineglasses. After he'd poured, he left the decanter on a low side table and exited the room. Lord Toppainsley, holding his glass by the stem, swirled the ruby liquid, then drew in a deep breath of its bouquet. Rafe and Tom did the same, although without the theatrics. As Rafe had known it would be, the wine was from the case he'd asked Jemmy Pratt to deliver earlier in the day.

"It's not every day that a wine like this lands on your doorstep." Toppainsley stuck his entire nose into the deep bowl of the glass.

"Manna from heaven," Rafe murmured, locking gazes with the man.

Sir Sibbald sipped judiciously. "Oh, this is excellent, my lord. What year is it?"

"Ninety-eight I believe. It was a very good year."

"For wine," Tom said. "Not for Bourbons."

Rafe chuckled. The wine the men were drinking

hadn't been in the bottle more than six months. Sir Sibbald, despite his appreciation for fine wines, clearly wasn't an expert.

The bottle was quickly emptied, but Toppainsley did not call for more. Instead, he announced that his wife had been feeling poorly lately, and was most likely tired. The dinner party was officially over. Standing, Rafe thought that it had never been a social event in the first place. He felt he'd peeled back the top layer of intrigue surrounding Toppainsley, but there were many more to go before he'd offer to sell the man some wine. After all, Toppainsley was Sir Sibbald's friend, and this little game of cat and mouse could easily be a trap.

In the ground floor foyer, servants had already draped the women in their outer-clothes. Goodbyes were warmly exchanged and the Toppainsleys received excessive praise from their guests on the quality of the dinner and the scintillating company.

"Hope to see you again," Lord Toppainsley said, vigorously shaking Rafe's hand. "Perhaps we can do business together in the near future."

For once, Rafe was at a loss for words, so thoroughly startled was he by Lord Toppainsley's brazen suggestion. Slanting a look at Sir Sibbald, who was admonishing Dovie that her pelisse was too thin for the frigid weather, Rafe quietly replied, "And what sort of business would that be, my lord?"

Sir Sibbald interrupted. "I haven't drunk such a fine wine in years, Topper! You must allow me to inspect your cellar some day."

Toppainsley smiled first at Rafe, then at Sir Sibbald. "I'm afraid you'll have to have a warrant, old man!"

Aloud, after giving Rafe a hearty slap on the back, Toppainsley said, "I'm interested in purchasing your house, of course. I had an ulterior motive in inviting you here, I confess. But, a gentleman mustn't discuss business in social environs, so I'll have my solicitor correspond with yours."

"I'm not interested in selling my house, my lord." Rafe smiled congenially, but his expression was unyielding. "For sentimental reasons. I'm certain you understand."

"Topper knows nothing of sentimentality," simpered Lady Toppainsley.

Everyone laughed politely. But, Rafe's smile faded as he stared at Rosalind. Waiting beside the door with her hands tucked in a fur muff, she stared boldly at him. If her ermine lined cloak didn't remind him of her privileged upbringing, her sullen little pout would have.

Lady Dovie, however, had eyes like a hawk. She cast Rafe a quelling glance, then grasped Rosalind's elbow and turned her toward the door. Sir Sibbald was quickly at his daughter's other side, his hand on her upper arm. But, Rosalind hung back until Rafe, having bid adieu to everyone else, was forced to speak to her.

"Good night, Miss Yardley." Rafe followed the Yardleys out of the door and walked behind them down the path that led to the street.

Over her father's shoulder, Rosalind said, "Good night, Rafe." Her use of his Christian name, and the tone of familiarity with which it rolled off her tongue, must have been a slap in Sir Sibbald's face.

Tom trotted halfway down the block to wake their sleeping carriage driver. Meanwhile, the Yardleys' gleaming black rig, fitted out with the latest in brass fixtures and lanterns, and drawn by some of the finest cattle Rafe had ever seen, stood waiting for its occupants. A dapper-looking tiger handed Lady Dovie into the carriage first, then reached for Miss Rosalind's hand.

As she withdrew one of her hands from her fur muff, she turned toward Rafe. "Here." She palmed the tiny object to him with such deftness that Rafe barely had time to blink before his gloved fingers closed around it. "I found this tucked inside my muff. It has your name engraved on it. The servants must have had a mix-up."

He managed to catch her fingertips before she withdrew. "Take care, Rosalind."

Sir Sibbald put a protective arm around his daughter's shoulders. "Come now, Rosie, it's cold out here."

The tiger assisted her and then her father into the carriage. A moment after it had rumbled off, Rafe's equipage appeared. He hopped into the icy interior and sat opposite Tom, who shivered beneath a thick lap blanket.

"What a bloody boring evening!" Tom said, his teeth chattering.

Rafe knocked on the ceiling hatch and gave instructions for the driver to turn toward the center of town. Given the mood he was in, the return trip to

Rye seemed unbearable at the moment. He needed a drink, something stronger than the fine Bordeaux he'd sampled at Lord Toppainsley's. And he needed some diversion, a vice, as it were, to occupy his mind. *Because he couldn't dispel the picture of Miss Rosalind Yardley's enticing little pout from his mind.* And because the ache he felt for her was becoming an insatiable itch. And because he'd just been handed evidence of her duplicity.

"Perhaps I was a bit precipitous in my judgment of Mrs. Simca's establishment." He opened his hand, displaying a silver object that glinted in the moonlight streaming through the carriage windows.

"What is that?" Tom asked.

"That, dear," Rafe replied grimly, "is my snuff box."

Rosalind sat before her father's imposing partner's desk. The atmosphere in Sir Sibbald's study was grave by design, but tonight the decor seemed particularly morbid. Staring at the stuffed game that dotted the dark paneled walls, Rosalind sympathized. Her father was a hunter at heart, and she was but a victim of his innate urge to conquer and control.

She squirmed beneath his disapproving stare. "I told you to forget about him. He is too old for you, dear, and too eccentric . . . and too . . ."

"Too far beneath me, Father?"

Sir Sibbald colored. "I didn't say that. He's titled, after all."

"He's titled, but he grew up poor. He married well,

extremely well, but he was never accepted by his wife's family. They looked down on him because he made a fortune in the shipping business."

"How do you know all that?"

"What do you think women do after dinner, Father, while the men smoke cigars and talk about politics? We talk about people—men, mostly, and tonight Rafe Lawless, Viscount Pershing, was the most interesting subject at hand."

"Lady Toppainsley said all those things?" Sir Sibbald looked confused. "Why would she concern herself with that man's background?"

"Perhaps she was attempting to dissuade me from being interested in him," Rosalind answered.

"She doesn't know you very well." There was some degree of affection in her father's voice, but his gaze remained stern. "In point of fact, she only succeeded in piquing your interest. Am I correct?"

Rosalind folded her arms across her chest.

"I want you to forget you ever met that man. That is my final pronouncement on the matter, and I'll brook no further argument from you."

"Lord and Lady Toppainsley like him."

"He isn't after Topper's daughter."

"Topper's daughter is one hundred years old, that's why."

Sir Sibbald frowned. "Besides, Lord Toppainsley wants to buy Lord Pershing's seaside house. He has no other interest in the man, I'm certain. Despite his pronouncement that he never mixes business in pleasure, that is the sole reason he invited the viscount and that overgrown moppet he calls a friend to his dinner party."

"Then why were *we* invited?" Sensing her father's hesitation, Rosalind stared hard at him. "I thought you adequately expressed your disapproval of the viscount at this week's ball. The Toppainsley's didn't have to include us in tonight's gathering. What's more, you didn't have to accept the invitation."

"You know how Topper is, Rosie. Well, if you don't, I'll tell you. His whole purpose in living seems to be giving parties and drinking. I'm quite certain he didn't appreciate the extent of my dislike for Rafe Lawless when he invited us all to dinner. And it would have been rude for me to refuse to go. It might even have been embarrassing for your stepmother. Oh, no, we had to go!"

Rosalind considered Sir Sibbald's answer. "I never have understood your connection with Lord Toppainsley. He's not your sort, Father. You have as much in common with him as you do with the viscount. Which is to say, nothing."

"That's not fair, Rosie."

"Face it, Father. This campaign against smuggling that you are on has turned you into a crusader. You've become enamored with your power and authority. You are judge, jury, and executioner all rolled up into one, and not just in matters of smuggling."

"That's not true! I highly resent that statement, and I demand an apology."

She pushed to the edge of her seat and gripped the arms of her chair with white knuckles. Years of pent-up anger spilled out of her, and even though she was appalled to hear what she was saying, she couldn't force shut the gates against her emotions. "You don't like Rafe Lawless, and you don't even have a good reason why! He's not like you, that's all. He's got a title, yes, and a better one than yours. But, he's not social enough, or well-liked enough, or politically influential enough—"

"He's not *anything* enough! Damme, child, don't you understand? I don't want you to marry some wandering Judas who has no roots, no family to speak of, no ties to the community. You're my daughter, Rosalind, and I've raised you to be a fine young lady. I want only the best for you, and I'll see that you get it even if you don't have the judgment to choose it for yourself."

"How dare you suggest that I am not capable of making that decision myself? Cover your ears, Father because I am about to say something very unpleasant. I don't care what you think about Rafe Lawless! I don't care whether you approve of my waltzing with him! I'm old enough to make my own decisions, and I'm going to make them as I see fit!"

"Not while you're living under my roof."

"Then, I'll leave." Rosalind's words came out in a torrent. Her frustration was so hot that her skin burned. "I'll go somewhere else. I'll get a job. I'll live with relatives. For God's sake, I'll find a protector if I have to."

Her father roared. "You'll do no such thing! And your mother would roll over in her grave if she heard you speak that way."

The mention of her mother made purple spots dance before Rosalind's eyes. "Mother may be turning over in her grave, but it's not because of my behavior."

Sir Sibbald blanched. His jaw moved, but no sound emerged from his lips. For a moment, stillness hung in the air. "Are you suggesting it is mine?" he finally croaked.

Through clenched teeth, Rosalind whispered, "How could you, Father? How could you marry that woman? She looks like a canary and talks like a parrot and thinks like a . . . like a pigeon!"

"I'll remind you, Rosalind, that is my wife you are speaking of."

"Mother was your wife! And you dishonored her by marrying Dovie! And you dishonored us both by letting Dovie hen-peck you the way she has! You used to be fun, Father. You used to laugh and smile and throw me up in the air and whirl me about. Then, Dovie came along, and suddenly, all you had time for was her. That silly, silly woman! I hate her!"

Sir Sibbald's fist slammed the top of his desk. A stack of business papers floated upward upon impact, then floated down into a haphazard pile. Leaning forward, Rosalind's father was as red and furious as she'd ever seen him. A streak of fear pulsed through her body, silencing her. She'd pushed him too far, and she'd wounded him. But, for all that she feared she'd driven her father to the brink of his patience, she couldn't bring herself to regret her words. He might lock her in a chastity belt and throw away the key in retribution for her insolence, but Rosalind

Yardley had said what she felt to him. She didn't feel good, but she did feel unburdened. And she was prepared for whatever punishment he might mete out to her now.

"You'll not leave this house, Rosalind. Not tonight, anyway," her father said in a strangely calm tone. He had pushed back in his chair, and though his face was still white as an ash tree, his expression was resolute. "I'll not have it said that a daughter of mine was denied the fundamentals of support, or turned out because we differed in opinion about something so silly as whom she should waltz with. But, if you feel so strongly about Dovie, then I expect you will want to be making other arrangements to live elsewhere. We have relatives in Kent who would love to take you in. Or I will make some arrangements for you and Mrs. Childress to return to London and set up household there. I really do love you, daughter, but I'm married to Dovie now and I have no intention of allowing you to injure her feelings any farther, or to ruin my marriage."

"You love her, don't you?" Rosalind's chest ached with the brutal knowledge of it. "You're choosing her over me, aren't you, Father?"

He met her gaze. He started to say something, but clamped his lips shut. Then, he half turned in his chair and looked away from her.

She thought he didn't want to see her, that she had become such an odious sight, he couldn't bear to look at her. Slowly, she stood, her heart pounding. The pain she felt was as palpable as a gunshot wound, and the sensation of rising to her full height, dizzying. What had transpired in the last few moments had changed the course of her life. She'd uttered the unspeakable, and she could never retrieve those words. And her father, true to his character, had refused to back down or to indulge her in her resentment toward Lady Dovie.

Her only choice was whether to depart now for a bucolic life in Kent, or to live the rest of her spinsterhood in residence with Lady Dovie, a woman whose antipathy Rosalind had been cultivating for years. Given that Sir Sibbald would assuredly repeat this bitter conversation word for word to Lady Dovie, Rosalind reckoned she might just as well start packing for the country.

"I'll leave before spring, Father," she said, turning away from him.

The fact he didn't argue nearly broke her heart.

Rafe sat in the crimson parlor at Mrs. Simca's, a shot glass of whiskey in his hand. Tom had encountered the leggy blond woman who favored fruit punches, and disappeared with her. Glancing at an ormolu clock perched on the mantelpiece, Rafe sighed impatiently. Mrs. Simca's establishment was quickly becoming his least favorite haunt.

At his elbow suddenly appeared an elegantly dressed woman.

"I am Mrs. Simca." She offered her hand.

As he stood, Rafe estimated the woman to be in her late fifties. She wore an impeccably tailored gown of gray taffeta and just enough precious gems on her neck and arms to suggest wealth but not gaudiness. Her upswept coiffure bespoke elaborate maintenance, yet it was neat and understated in the style of Beau Brummel. And, while there was something alluringly feminine about this doyenne of the demireps, she had the keen gaze of a businessman and as much self-confidence as any aristocrat Rafe had ever encountered.

Noting the firmness of her handshake, he quickly concluded that any attempt to pull the wool over Mrs. Simca's eyes would be ill-advised. "I admit, I was curious to meet you."

Her lips curved upward. "Most men are surprised when they do. Did you expect an aging tabby, with a wrinkled bosom and too much rouge on my face?"

Rafe found himself chuckling. Mrs. Simca beckoned for more whiskey and bade him to sit down. She settled in a plush armchair catty-corner from him and sipped a small glass of brandy.

"What can I do for you?"

"My name is Rafe Lawless—"

"Viscount Pershing. I know who you are."

He paused, startled. *Perhaps Tom told her who he was.*

She smiled. "Don't trouble yourself with my sources of intelligence, my lord. In my business, it is imperative that I know who I am dealing with. For the safety and welfare of my girls, you understand."

He swallowed hard. "There was a woman here the other night. Her name is Adelaide."

"Baby?" Mrs. Simca's perfectly shaped brows shot up.

"I'd like to see her."

"She's, er, unavailable at the moment. Perhaps you'd like to meet another girl. Penelope is very young—"

"No, I want to see Adelaide. It's very important, Mrs. Simca."

"She's not working tonight. I'm sorry, my lord, that I am unable to satisfy your needs. Come back in about two weeks. Perhaps Baby will be available then."

"Where is she? Why can't I see her tonight?"

Mrs. Simca rose in a rustle of taffeta and indignation. "That is none of your concern."

Rafe stood toe to toe with her. He spoke in a low tone so as not to disturb the other couples in the room, but his voice was thick with tension. "Something has happened to her, hasn't it?"

"Why are you asking, my lord?"

"Because I lost my snuffbox here, and it was returned to me by a young woman. Someone gave her the snuff box and asked her to pass it to me. 'Twas a message of sorts. I want to know who the message was from."

"Why don't you ask this young woman who gave her the snuffbox?"

"She doesn't know. She found it hidden inside her fur muff."

Mrs. Simca's expression hardened. "The symbolism is amusing, my lord. Nevertheless, Adelaide cannot speak with you tonight. She took a rather nasty tumble and broke her nose."

"Someone hurt her." Rafe's fists coiled at his sides. "One of your esteemed patrons beat the devil out of her, didn't he? Who was it, Mrs. Simca? Tell me, I must know."

"I have my own way of dealing with these sorts of matters, my lord. I do not need your assistance, however chivalrous your impulse may be."

He felt like shaking the woman, but somehow Rafe knew that if he laid a finger on her, her team of trained bouncers would materialize and he'd be tossed out on the street within a flash. "I strongly recommend you cooperate with me, Mrs. Simca. Whoever injured Adelaide may very well be the same individual who took my snuffbox."

She gave him a long, measuring look. At length, she said, "She's upstairs. You may visit with her for five minutes. That's all. Then I must ask you to leave, my lord. And I would greatly appreciate it if you would never return."

"You have no need to worry on that score, Mrs. Simca."

Rafe followed the woman up the stairs to Adelaide's room. Mrs. Simca knocked lightly on the door.

A weak voice responded, "Come in."

"Five minutes," Mrs. Simca said, pushing open the door.

Rafe slipped into the darkened room. A single taper guttered on the bedside table. As his eyes adjusted to the dim lighting, a sickening rage twisted in Rafe's gut. Beneath a mountain of blankets lay Adelaide, her face bruised, her nose misshapen. Whoever had beaten her had done so with the ferocity of an animal. If Rafe ever got his hands on the man . . .

When he emerged from Adelaide's bedchamber five minutes later, his head throbbed and his eyes stung with unshed tears. He nodded at Mrs. Simca, and she nodded back wordlessly. They had an understanding. Rafe would never return to this place. As he walked the long corridor to the staircase, he was aware that Mrs. Simca slipped into Adelaide's room behind him, perhaps to comfort her employee, perhaps to protect her investment. Rafe felt a stab of disgust. He had no use for a woman who trafficked in flesh, even if she reeked of gentility and grace. Adelaide's fate made him even more determined to take control of his own.

Ten

The small dining room in The Cockeyed Rooster was bustling with business. Given that the inn was situated on the edge of town, it was a popular rest point for travelers, farmers, purveyors and highwaymen alike. Assaulted with the odor of frying sausages mingled with unwashed bodies, Rosalind wrinkled her nose. Mrs. Childress linked a protective arm around her charge's waist as the proprietress led them to a small corner table.

Rosalind and Mrs. Childress sat, careful to avoid wiping the greasy tabletop with their sleeves.

"My name's Miz Sawyer, dearie." The woman wiped a grimy towel across the surface of the table. "What would you two ladies like to eat for breakfast?"

"I'd like a cup of tea and some pastries," Rosalind replied.

"Got some raisin scones," Mrs. Sawyer said. "And you, dearie?"

Mrs. Childress looked around at the heaping plates on her neighbor's table. "The sausages look good. And I'll have some jam and biscuits."

When the proprietress was gone, the governess said, "If your father knew what you were about, he'd have my head on a platter, Rosie. We'd best eat quickly and get home before he realizes we've gone missing."

"He thinks we're shopping, Mrs. C."

"Then we'd best return with some packages."

Rosalind sighed. Her governess was right. If her father ever caught wind of what she was up to, or what she'd done, he'd send her to Kent without waiting for her to pack her belongings. But, the thought that she'd shot a man, perhaps crippled him for life, or worse, haunted her. If Lord Pershing refused to tell her where to find Redd Fellowes, she'd have to track him down herself.

"Have you ever done something so wrong, Mrs. C., that you knew you just had to put it at rights, or you wouldn't be able to live with yourself?"

"You didn't intentionally injure anyone, Rosie. Lord Pershing told you he would take care of the man, and it is his responsibility to do so. Under the circumstances, I hold him liable for this Mr. Fellowes's misfortune, not you."

"It was my finger that pulled the trigger."

"It was Lord Pershing who got you into that bumblebroth. Let him make amends to Mr. Fellowes."

Rosalind shook her head. A serving girl appeared with a pot of hot tea and two cracked cups. When she was gone, Rosalind lifted the cup to her lips, allowing the steam to warm her face. "It's as if my entire life has been spent inside a prison, Mrs. C."

"A prison? Child, you don't know what you're talking about. You haven't known a day of hardship! Yes, I know how you feel about Lady Dovie. The entire household, including Dovie, knows now. You made that quite clear last night. But, you're being a mite melodramatic, Rosie, if you say you've suffered a hard life."

"Alright, then, not the sort of prison where a person is deprived of the comforts of life. I'm talking about a different kind of prison. I've been deprived of the privilege of making my own decisions, Mrs. C. Up till now, every thing I've done, every friend I've chosen, and every man I've spoken to, was part of a carefully constructed plan. A plan that was meant to lead to my living happily forever after."

"What's wrong with that?"

"It was my father's plan, that's what's wrong."

Mrs. Childress spoke to her as if she were a slow child. "Your father loves you. He only wants the best for you."

"He doesn't know me." Rosalind paused as the servant girl covered the tabletop with plates of sausages, eggs, biscuits, and sweet breads. A tub of freshly churned butter and small crock of jam complimented the savory fare. Slathering a scone with the sweet butter, Rosalind added, "And he doesn't know what will make me happy."

"Do you?" Mrs. Childress asked around a mouthful of sausage.

"Maybe not. But, I'm going to find out. And if I make a mistake, then it's my mistake."

"And damn the consequences," Mrs. Childress whispered, although the patrons of The Cockeyed

Rooster would most likely not be shocked to hear a woman utter such a vulgarity.

"Father didn't take my needs into consideration when he married Lady Dovie. Why should I protect his tender sensibilities now?"

"Let me understand this, Rosie. Precisely what do you propose to do now that you've declared your independence from your father? Do you have a scheme for achieving this lofty goal of personal satisfaction? Do you have a specific goal, such as marrying the most unsuitable reprobate you can find? Or is your aim more generalized in that you simply intend to do all that you can to defy your father?"

Her governess's facetious tone rankled. But Rosalind knew the woman had her best interests at heart, and so she bit back the sharp words that sprang to her tongue. Instead, she said, "Mrs. C., I intend to find Redd Fellowes and make amends for what I have done. Because the first step in achieving my independence is to take responsibility for my mistakes. Don't you see? I know I can't erase the mistakes I've made in the past. *But I can own them.* And I can admit to them. And then, I can atone for them."

"Do you expect Mr. Fellowes to forgive you?"

"No. It's forgiveness from myself that I am looking for."

Mrs. Childress looked heavenward. "Why don't you just go to church, dearie?"

"Because God helps those who help themselves. And I'm going to be a better person than the cosseted little brat my father raised. I'm certain he thought he was protecting me all these years, Mrs. C., but now

I've got to be a grown-up. I've got to do what I think is right, regardless of the consequences."

"I hope I'll like living in Kent," the governess murmured.

"And when I've taken responsibility for my mistakes, then I can take responsibility for my happiness, too."

"Oh, so this is where the reprehensible rogue comes into the picture!"

Rosalind smiled. When she caught Mrs. Sawyer's eye, she raised her hand and waved her over. The older woman toddled to the table with an expression of concern. "What's the matter, dearie, didna' like the sausages?"

"No, they're fine." Rosalind waggled her fingers in the air, desperate for a *serviette*. Seeing none, she resisted the urge to wipe her greasy fingers on Mrs. Sawyer's apron. "I wonder if you could answer a question for me. I'm looking for a man named Redd Fellowes."

"Never heard of him."

"Are you certain? If you know where he is, I would pay you for the information."

"If I knew, gel, I would tell you. I can always use a little extra money in me pocket."

"You might have seen him in the company of a Rafe Lawless, Viscount Pershing."

The woman's expression changed instantly. Her eyes were two little nuggets in her potato face, and her jowls trembled as she spoke. "Said I didna' know him. And that's all I got to say. Now, if you're finished with your meal, I'd thank ye to pay me and leave. There's other folk wantin' to sit down and eat."

Their dismissal was so abrupt that Rosalind's cheeks burned with humiliation. Heads turned and stared as she and Mrs. Childress stalked through the tiny dining room with their chins held up and their backs stiff as pokers. In the carriage, Rosalind cleaned her fingers on the lap blanket and sulked. Repenting for her sins was turning out to be more complicated than she'd envisioned. Her mission to find Redd Fellowes was beginning to feel like a wild-goose chase.

Halfway back to Brighton, Mrs. Childress dared to interrupt the chilly silence. "Are you prepared to forget about this Redd Fellowes fellow now? For your own sake, child?"

Rosalind folded her arms across her chest, and replied bitterly, "No, in fact, I've decided to take a different tack. Perhaps this Mr. Fellowes keeps a low profile because he is involved in illegal activities. If that is the case, then only one man will be able to tell me where he is."

"Lord Pershing has already refused to divulge that information to you."

"Then, I've only one alternative. I've got to change his mind."

"And how do you intend to do that?"

Rosalind bit her lip. She knew the man had a weakness for her. Despite his coldness toward her at the Toppainsleys, he was vulnerable to her charms. She knew he'd been warned off her, and that he'd resolved to leave her alone. And she didn't doubt his determination or his iron will.

But, men were lusty creatures, after all. He might think himself impervious to Rosalind's charms, but he hadn't encountered the full array of her feminine wiles.

Whatever that meant. In her state of virginal innocence, Rosalind could only imagine the things a woman might do to seduce a man. But, those imaginings were wicked and delicious. Snug beneath her lap blanket, a shiver of excitement ran through her body.

Mrs. Childress's concern was evident by the puzzled frown on her face. But, as the governess had said, *consequences be damned.* Miss Rosalind Yardley was on a mission. She tapped the ceiling door, and when it opened, instructed the driver to head toward Rye. Mrs. Childress gasped, but said nothing. Clearly, the woman realized any remonstrations or protests would be useless. *Rosalind was making her own decisions now.*

Seated in his drawing room before the fireplace, drinking tepid coffee, Rafe stared absently into the roaring flames. Depression overwhelmed him. Not since Annette's illness had he felt so angry or bitter.

With the buzz of caffeine roaring through his veins, he tried to make sense of the previous week's events. His initial encounter with Miss Rosalind Yardley had knocked him off balance. Her pluck that night on the beach, and her brazenness later that evening in his house, intrigued him. His physical attraction to her was so strong and so feral that it frightened him. Even in the first days of his marriage to Annette, when he'd been wildly in love with his wife, he'd never experienced the sensation of being out of control.

Yet, when Rafe kissed Rosalind in the wee hours of the morning during their carriage ride to Brighton, something had snapped inside him. Or, perhaps he was simply going insane.

His next place of residence would be Bedlam, he thought, sipping his coffee. No man in his right mind would continue to obsess over a woman whose father had the power to ruin his life. The fact that Sir Sibbald had point-blank told Rafe to leave Rosalind alone added ammunition to the argument that he was crazy not to. It didn't matter, though. Rafe couldn't cease thinking about her, wondering what she was doing, where she was, and how she was feeling.

He dropped his head in his hand and rubbed his eyes. On the table beside him gleamed the cursed little snuffbox he'd left at Mrs. Simca's. Looking at it pained him. The mystery surrounding Rosalind's possession of it caused his brain to ache and his gut to twist. Adelaide's whispered story had solved only a tiny piece of the puzzle, but the overall picture was as blurred as a watercolor left in the rain.

He didn't hear Tom enter the drawing room. "He says he's never heard of Mrs. Simca, much less a woman named Baby. Or even Adelaide."

Rafe's head popped up. "Do you believe him?"

Tom detoured to the sideboard, grabbed a bottle of whiskey and a glass, then slouched in the chair opposite Rafe's. "I don't know what to believe." He poured a stiff drink and threw it back in one gulp. "He fits the description Adelaide gave you."

"Down to the very last detail."

"But she didn't know his name."

"The man who beat her called himself Mr. Brown. Said he was from Leeds, and that he made his money in coal. She had no reason to doubt him. Mrs. Simca said he had outstanding references."

"Still, how do you suppose this Mr. Brown got your snuffbox?" Tom's glass slipped from his fingers and landed with a thud on the carpet. He swigged directly from the bottle after that.

Eyeing his friend with some concern, Rafe replied, "She admitted to stealing it. When she sat down, she felt the box beneath her thigh. When we stood, she closed her fingers around it. I never noticed."

"Hardly surprising, given the circumstances."

"Poor thing. I can't even be angry that she'd pilfer my snuffbox. I feel responsible for her injuries."

"So do I." Tom took another healthy gulp. "I was the one who urged you to go there in the first place. Had I kept my mouth shut, Adelaide would never have been hurt."

"You're taking this too hard, Tom. Slow down on the whiskey."

Ignoring his friend's warning, Tom said, in slightly slurred speech, "Do you think this Mr. Brown, however he is, saw you leave the drawing room with Adelaide? Was he there at Mrs. Simca's the entire time you were?"

"I suppose that's a possibility." Rafe tried to picture the other men in the crimson parlor the night he met Adelaide, but it was impossible to distinguish any faces. The room was purposely set up to provide privacy for the customers, and the lighting was so dim, he could have brushed Tom's elbow in passing and not recognized him.

"I worked him over pretty good, Rafe. He might be lying, but if he is, he's a bloody good liar."

"You didn't break any bones, did you?"

Shuddering violently, Tom said, "No."

"We've got to believe he's innocent until we can prove otherwise," Rafe said through clenched teeth. "Despite Adelaide's description of Mr. Brown."

"Hard to believe there's another man as ugly as Jemmy Pratt," Tom said hoarsely, before he dipped forward and his snoring eclipsed his groggy speech.

Rafe, miserable and weary, drained his glass and set it aside. If he couldn't achieve the mind-numbing senselessness Tom had opted for, at least he could catch a few moments of sleep. He squeezed shut his eyes, willing himself to forget about Rosalind.

What part did she play in the intrigue surrounding the return of his snuffbox?

Was her motivation evil? Was she working for her father, Sir Sibbald?

A dozen theories, all of them sinister, swirled in Rafe's mind. When the sound of carriage wheels outside the house intruded on his meandering thoughts, he whispered a salty curse. His life was spinning out of control. His emotions were hopelessly jumbled. And every action he took added speed to his downward spiral.

* * *

"There's a young lady and her governess here to see you, my lord."

The butler's pronouncement startled Rafe awake. His eyes flew open. He didn't know how long he'd been sleeping, but Tom's snoring had ceased to disturb him long ago. Reaching over, he gave his friend a vigorous shake.

As Rosalind Yardley Mrs. Childress entered the drawing room, Tom scrubbed his face with his hands and gave a wide-mouthed yawn. "What time is it?"

Standing, Rafe said, "Time for you to go, old man. I have company."

Tom scrambled to his feet. At the sight of Rosalind, standing primly in the middle of the floor, he blushed and scratched his head. "I was just going," he said, backing out of the room.

"Strange young man," Mrs. Childress muttered.

"Well!" Taken off guard, Rafe awkwardly gestured to the same sofa that he and Rosalind had fallen on the night he met her. The memory of that first encounter pulsed through him like lightning. Fully awake, and aware of his disheveled appearance, he ran his fingers through his thick hair, and said, "Can I offer you ladies some tea?"

"No, thank you," Rosalind said. "We're here on business."

"Strictly business," Mrs. Childress chimed in.

The crispness in their voices chafed the air. Rafe stood before the fireplace, one arm propped on the mantelpiece. "What sort of business, Miss Yardley?"

"I want to know where I can find Redd Fellowes."

A beat passed before Rafe realized who she was talking about. It was the fictional victim of her errant gunshot. Redd Fellowes had been Rafe's sword of Damocles, the leverage he used to persuade her that telling her father where she'd been the night she went missing was a bad idea. "You're looking for Mr. Fellowes, are you?"

"Don't stall, Lord Pershing." She was as beautiful as she was the night he kissed her, perhaps more so with her pink cheeks and glittering blue eyes. "Just tell me where I can find him."

That was going to be tricky. Rafe rubbed his chin. "You can't see him. It's impossible."

"Why?"

"Because he's . . . because he's recovering from his injuries. In an undisclosed location. A safe place where no one will disturb him. Believe me, Rosalind—I mean, Miss Yardley—it's for the best. I didn't want anyone asking difficult questions. And when a man gets shot, for God's sake, well, there are inevitably going to be questions asked."

"By whom?" Rosalind asked.

"Well, by the authorities, for one. And the surgeon who treated him. That's why I had to tuck him away in a country hideaway. Paid the doctor a fortune not to report the shooting incident to the sheriff. But, it was necessary to protect you."

"Protect me?" Her mouth formed a little O.

Looking as grave as possible, Rafe said, "That was the bargain we made, wasn't it? I would protect you from the repercussions of your crime, and you wouldn't report mine to your father. One hand washes another, isn't that the saying?"

"You can forget all that, I'm afraid. You see, I've had a change of heart. I no longer want your protection or your paternalism. I'm ready to admit that I caused injury to this man, and if I have to admit it publicly to flush him out, I will."

Horror gripped Rafe's heart, but he forced himself to continue smiling. It was a fraudulent smile that caused his facial muscles to ache, but he couldn't allow Rosalind to know how much her pronouncement terrified him. "But, Miss Yardley, a public admission that you shot a man would ruin your social career. It would destroy your chances of marriage, and ban you from the most exclusive salons in Mayfair and Brighton."

"I don't care."

"Your father would be devastated."

She absorbed that remark with some degree of concern. Her pretty little forehead creased and she shot a quick questioning look in Mrs. Childress's direction. "He'll survive. My own integrity is more important."

What had gotten into this girl? Where was the spoiled daddy's girl who waltzed with Rafe a few nights ago? Was this part of her scheme to defy her father? Was she merely trying to get Sir Sibbald's attention by shocking the old man out of his moribund senses?

"I applaud your forthrightness, Miss Yardley. But the fact remains, I am not going to tell you where Mr. Fellowes is."

"You must." She leaned forward, her hands twisting the velvet braid strap of a black kid reticule. "I've got to make amends to the man. I've injured him, rendered him a cripple, perhaps. His family could be starving, for all I know, while I am living comfortably beneath my father's roof, without a care in the world. It wouldn't be fair! It wouldn't be right!"

Rafe's heart squeezed at the sight of her, so intense, so earnest. Could she possibly be so remorseful for her actions that she wanted to find Red Fellowes and make recompense to him?

Mrs. Childress cleared her throat. "Might I have a drop of brandy, my lord?"

Grateful for the distraction, Rafe crossed the room and rummaged in the sideboard for another bottle of liquor. He poured Mrs. Childress a generous drink and handed it to her. When she'd taken a lusty gulp, she sighed and licked her lips. "Thank you. Now, since I'm charged with the responsibility for looking after Miss Yardley, I'd like to say a word."

Relief poured through Rafe's body; surely, the governess would exercise good sense by telling Rosalind to forget about Mr. Fellowes.

"I think you'd best tell Miss Yardley what you know about this Fellowes character." The older woman's lips formed a straight line.

Rafe's heart dropped like a stone.

"She has a right to know," Mrs. Childress continued. "I dare say, I am favorably impressed by Rosalind's determination in this respect. I wouldn't have believed she had it in her if I hadn't seen it myself!"

"Hallelujah. I am delighted that Miss Yardley has

finally sprouted scruples." *Why did it have to be now?*
"But, I can't tell you where Mr. Fellowes is . . . because I don't know."

Rosalind bristled like an angry cat. "I resent your facetiousness. And I don't believe you. You didn't say that before!"

"Well, I'm telling you now. I don't know where he is."

The double doors of the drawing room opened, and Tom entered, briskly crossing the room to stand beside Rafe at the mantelpiece. "Excuse me, but did I hear you discussing the whereabouts of Redd Fellowes?"

"You did." Rafe stared at him.

"I believe I might be able to offer some assistance." Tom wore a very serious expression.

"Go on," Rafe bit out.

"He shipped out yesterday to the West Indies."

Rosalind's face lit up. "Yesterday? The West Indies? Are you certain?"

Tom stroked his chin and looked pensive. "Quite certain. So, you see, Mr. Fellowes won't return for many months."

"Was he well enough to endure such a long sea journey?" Rosalind questioned.

"Quite," Tom replied. "He's a tough bird. I wouldn't worry about him."

"Oh, but I am worried!" Rosalind's fingers twisted the cord in her lap. "The man was seriously injured, yet he took a position on a ship heading toward the West Indies . . . well, he must have a family to support. I can think of no other reason a man would subject himself to that sort of punishment."

"The wound wasn't as serious as we first thought," Tom stammered. " 'Twas only a flesh wound, really."

Rafe shifted his weight. "I was unaware you knew so much about Mr. Fellowes's condition."

Tom smiled at him. "Just trying to be helpful."

"And you are being helpful." Rosalind stood, a look of purpose on her face. "Do you know what ship he sailed on?"

Confident, Tom answered, "I believe it was *The Windsong.*"

"*The Windsong.*" For the first time since she'd entered Rafe's house, Rosalind smiled brightly. "Well, that is a stroke of luck. If I am not mistaken, my father's friend Lord Toppainsley owns that ship. He'll know whether Mr. Redd Fellowes was aboard, and what condition he was in. More importantly, he'll be able to tell me how to find the man's family. Perhaps they need money. I'm certain they do!"

Mrs. Childress pushed off the settee and took her young charge's elbow. "Come, dear, we have much to do."

Rosalind was in such a hurry to leave, she barely glanced at Rafe. "Good day, my lord." Linking her arm in her governess's, she turned and headed toward the door.

"Wait—" Tom took a step forward.

Rafe suppressed his laughter. Tom's attempt to quell Rosalind's quest had backfired.

The women paused.

"Was there something else you remembered?" Rosalind asked.

Shrugging, Tom waved his hands in the air, clearly desperate for something to say. "You'd be wasting your time if you tried to run Mr. Fellowes's family to ground. They've returned to Wales, you see, to live with relatives until the head of their household returns. Which could be months, or even years, if I know Redd. A regular wanderlust, he is. Unpredictable, irresponsible, and thoroughly incorrigible. A completely irredeemable jackanapes. Wouldn't waste a second of my time on him if I were you."

Rosalind gave him a tight smile. "All the more reason to look up his family. If he's that irresponsible, they'll welcome any help I can give them."

"She's got to make amends," warbled Mrs. Childress.

"Foolish girl!" Rafe's temper exploded. "You're going to get yourself in trouble. You're meddling in things you know nothing about. Go home to your father, Rosalind, and stay there—for your own safety and welfare!"

Releasing Mrs. Childress, Rosalind whirled. She closed the distance between herself and Rafe, standing toe to toe with him, staring up at his obsidian gaze. His body reverberated with tension and barely suppressed violence, but Rosalind was fearless. She knew the man wouldn't harm her. He might be a cruel rogue, but he was not the sort of man to hit a woman.

No, it was *her* anger that frightened her. Rosalind struggled against the urge to strike Rafe's face.

"Go on, slap me," he whispered.

His voice had the raspy depth of intimacy. An erotic thrill rippled up Rosalind's spine, heightening her anger and her fear. Behind her, Mrs. Childress gasped and Tom stammered something, but Rafe threw up his hands, and without taking his gaze off Rosalind, said, "Leave us alone."

"I can't do that!" cried Mrs. Childress. "I'm responsible for her!"

"Get her out of here!" Rafe's command boomed through the house, rattling the very rafters and joists that held it together.

Though Rosalind's gaze was locked with Rafe's, she knew that Tom had taken Mrs. Childress by the arm and guided her toward the door. "It's alright," she said quietly. "I'll be fine, Mrs. C."

The older woman's protests could be heard even as the double doors clicked shut. Then, Rosalind stood in deafening silence mere inches from the viscount. His nearness was overwhelming. The aroma surrounding him—a mixture of liquor, soap, leather, and perspiration—was intoxicating. The sheer animal maleness he exuded was powerfully arousing.

Swallowing hard, Rosalind realized she'd never seen her father this angry, this *aggressive*. She didn't know whether she should be repulsed or attracted; in truth, she felt a little of both.

"How do you know Toppainsley owns *The Windsong*?" he growled.

"Give Lady Toppainsley a little treacle, and she's as garrulous as a Methodist preacher."

His gaze scanned her face, drawing patches of heat

to her cheeks. She searched his eyes, but didn't know whether he was repulsed or attracted to her. The same mixture of desire and mistrust that she felt in her heart was cruelly reflected in his stone-cold expression. Yet, his breathing was ragged and his slightly parted lips appeared hungry for hers.

He grasped her upper arms. "Go home, little girl."

His touch thrilled her. His strong fingers, grappling her woolen cloak and tightening around her muscles, held her in a sort of weightless rapture. "What if I refuse to go home?"

"You're playing with fire, don't you understand?"

"I know what I'm about. Don't patronize me," she whispered. "I'll hate you if you do."

His eyes shut tightly for a moment. When he opened them, there was a sparkle on his thick lashes, and a wounded look in his gaze. Through a clenched jaw, he said, "You would hate me sooner or later, Rosalind. I am not the man for you. I can't give you all that you're accustomed to, nor do I care to spend the remainder of my life trying. If I failed again, I would—"

She didn't know what he was talking about, but his anguish was palpable. And so was the ferocity of his emotion. As his fingers closed tighter around her arm, Rosalind gasped. "You're hurting me."

Startled, he released her. But as she swayed backward, he quickly enveloped her in his arms, hugging her tightly and whispering, "I'm sorry. I would never hurt you."

Pressing her palms against his muscled chest, Rosalind pushed Rafe to arm's length so that she could look at him. Confusion assailed her. The man she'd first viewed as the symbol of her independence now held her enthralled, entrapped, and imprisoned. In her efforts to escape her father's paternalism, she'd become captivated by another man, a man more powerful and frightening than any she'd ever met. Had she simply traded one protector for another?

Rosalind's views of liberation and freedom tilted topsy-turvy. But while her mind spun, her body ached for Rafe's embrace. And she knew there wasn't much time. It wouldn't be long before Mrs. Childress overrode Tom Wickham's objections and burst into the room to defend her virtue.

"Kiss me," she said.

Half-lidded and wolf-hungry, his gaze was fixed on her lips. But he said, "No," as if the word was wrenched from his gut, and took a step backward, gripping the edge of the mantelpiece.

His rejection felt like a battering ram to the stomach. Reeling and breathless, Rosalind could only stare at him, wondering what she'd done wrong and why this man refused to kiss her. Perhaps he truly was repulsed by her. Perhaps he was still obsessed by the memory of his deceased wife. Perhaps he was in love with another woman.

The possibilities were endless, but they all boiled down to one thing: he didn't love her, and he never would.

Inching backward, Rosalind fought to maintain her composure. She loved Rafe Lawless, Viscount Pershing, and she was prepared to admit it. It didn't matter that her attraction to him was mixed up with the conflict she had with her father. It didn't matter that the thrall Rafe held her in was inexplicably intense and dangerously emotional, perhaps even obsessive and slightly twisted. She loved him, deeply and wholly. She loved his power and his melancholy, his single-mindedness and his eccentricity. She loved the fact he didn't care what society thought of him. And she loved the fact he was afraid of nothing.

"I promised your father I would leave you alone."

Stunned, Rosalind felt a coldness in her blood. "I don't believe you. I mean, I don't believe that is why you refuse to kiss me."

He looked at her then, hard. The house on the cliff creaked and moaned against the buffeting winds, but inside that drawing room, the air was as still as granite. "You're quite right, Rosalind. It has nothing to do with your father. It's me. You don't know me. You don't want to know me."

"Yes, I do."

With a heavy sigh, he averted his gaze. He picked up an iron poker and jabbed the ashy faggots in the fireplace. The fire had dwindled, giving head to the chill that blanketed the room. "Alright, then. I don't want to know you, Rosalind. How's that? I don't want to know what you like or don't like. I don't want to know what makes you happy or sad. I don't want to know you intimately, Rosalind, because—"

He halted, hating himself for what he said. How could he tell Rosalind that he didn't want to love her because he was afraid he couldn't make her happy? How could he tell her he lacked the courage to love her?

How could he tell her he was an outlaw whose future held nothing more certain than a free passage to Australia?

Unable to tell her the truth, Rafe turned his back to her. "Go away, little girl," he repeated so harshly that his own skin rippled with disgust.

Eleven

"I *know* Father would not approve." Rosalind took her governess's hand and pulled her up the path that led to the Toppainsley's town house.

"It's not right, our ambushing the man like this. Besides, I doubt if he has any of his business records here."

"We're making a friendly social call," Rosalind said, banging the brass knocker on the door. "Nothing unusual about that."

"What if he's not at home?"

"Then we'll get whatever information we can from Lady Toppainsley."

The door opened to the sight of a smiling footman clad in resplendent satin livery fit for Prinny's staff. Rosalind politely announced that she and Mrs. Childress had come to pay a visit on Lady Toppainsley. Once inside the foyer, she slipped her calling card into the footman's gloved hand. After he ushered her into the drawing room, he backed out and vanished. Seconds later, a serving girl appeared with tea, and shortly afterward, Lady Toppainsley breezed into the room.

"What a lovely surprise!" In her old-fashioned hoop skirts, she perched awkwardly on the edge of a love seat.

Rosalind thought she looked like Marie Antoinette. "I wanted to tell you how much I enjoyed your dinner party."

Lady Toppainsley looked a bit confused. "How sweet. I'm sorry Lady Dovie couldn't accompany you today."

"Actually, she doesn't know we're here." Rosalind flashed a winning smile. "Is Lord Toppainsley at home today? I should like very much to compliment him on the excellent dinner that was served. And Father hasn't ceased ranting about the fine Bordeaux he drank, and the fine port."

"Topper is out for the afternoon, dear." Lady Toppainsley looked thoroughly bewildered now. It was odd enough that Rosalind and her governess would drop in for a visit without Lady Dovie. That Rosalind wished to see Lord Toppainsley was strange indeed.

"Oh." Rosalind's face fell. "When will he return?"

"Er, I don't know, child. But, I will tell him came for a visit. He'll be most pleased to hear you enjoyed the dinner party."

Standing, Rosalind replied, "Perhaps if I return later this afternoon?"

"Whatever for?" All three women were standing now, and Lady Toppainsley's consternation was evident. Apparently, she didn't like the idea of Rosalind wanting so badly to see her husband.

Rosalind suddenly realized that she'd given the wrong impression. Eager to correct Lady Toppainsley's misapprehension, she said, "Forgive me. To be honest, I wanted to ask his lordship a question. About a ship he owns called *The Windsong*. I think there is a crew member on the ship whose family requires assistance."

"I don't understand, dear." Lady Toppainsley's concern had abated, but she remained thoroughly confused.

"Just tell him I want to talk about *The Windsong*." Rosalind was eager to leave, having realized her *faux pas*. "And, please, my lady, don't tell Lady Dovie about this conversation."

"This is very strange." Lady Toppainsley looked at Mrs. Childress for some explanation, but the governess only shrugged and lifted her brows.

As the women walked toward the door, Lady Toppainsley said, "Well, if you want to talk with my husband so badly, it's a shame you'll not be attending the dance we are giving tomorrow evening."

"Another party?" blurted Mrs. Childress.

"Why not?" Lady Toppainsley's tone evoked the sentiment, *Let them eat cake*.

"Why not, indeed?" Rosalind was sick to death of the Toppainsley's parties, but the opportunity to quiz Lord Toppainsley was too tempting to ignore. "I'll be there."

"Your parents are slated to attend, but Dovie informed me that Sir Sibbald felt you'd attended too many festivities of late."

"You know Father. When I tell him how badly I want to attend, he'll bend to my will."

"Fathers are like that," Lady Toppainsley simpered.

"Oh, dear, another party." Mrs. Childress's distress was tangible. She gripped Rosalind's elbow and rushed her down the steps and through the foyer.

Lady Toppainsley stood at the landing staring down at them. She waggled her pale fingers and cooed good-bye.

But, as soon as the doors closed behind her unexpected guests, her smile vanished. Gathering her skirts, she stomped back up the steps and stormed into her husband's study.

Seated behind his desk, a ledger splayed open in front of him, he looked up in surprise. His wife marched forward wearing a warrior's expression beneath her mask of almond paste. The little black beauty mole she'd painted at the corner of her lips twitched convulsively.

Removing his reading glasses, Lord Toppainsley said, "Whatever is the matter, love?"

"It's that Yardley chit. Really, Topper, I'm afraid this entire little scheme of yours is going to explode in our faces."

"What about Rosalind Yardley?"

"She just showed up to pay a visit."

"Nothing unusual about that."

"With her governess, and without Lady Dovie."

Lord Toppainsley made a moue of unconcern. "So?"

"It was a ruse, Topper. She had no interest in doing

the pretty with me. What she really wanted was to talk with you."

He looked puzzled. "About what?"

"She wants to ask you some questions about *The Windsong*."

"*The Windsong*? What could she possibly know about my shipping business?"

"Either Sir Sibbald is playing you for a fool, or else this parvenu Lord Pershing is angling to put *you* out of business. I don't know which it is, but she's clearly delivering a message of sorts. She probably doesn't even know that she's being used."

"Sibbald wouldn't use his daughter in that manner. It must be Pershing. He's onto me, and he's letting me know that if I move into his territory, he'll expose me."

"Why would he do that? You could just as easily expose his criminal activities."

"Maybe. Maybe not." A moment passed during which Lord Toppainsley tilted his head and nibbled the stem of his spectacles. He scratched his bald pate. Without his powdered wig, his head felt itchy and naked. Then, he slowly looped the wire-framed glasses over his ears, and returned his gaze to the open ledger. "Don't worry, dear. I'll take care of it."

"She's going to be at our party tomorrow night."

His lips curled. "Wonderful. Then, I believe we should invite Rafe, Lord Pershing, as well."

Lady Toppainsley's breathing returned to normal. Her husband knew how to handle things. Leaving his presence, she began to fret over what gown she would wear the following night, and which jewels she would drape on her body. To hell with that nosey little Miss Rosalind Yardley. She'd get her comeuppance before long. Her interference was no longer Lady Toppainsley's concern.

As long as her husband—*Topper, as she affectionately called him*—was in control, Lady Toppainsley's confectionary world of parties and taffeta and fist-sized emeralds would never end.

"He's refusing to pay, Rafe!" Tom slammed the carriage door behind him, then threw himself on the leather squabs opposite Rafe.

The viscount sighed. "What reason did he give?"

"Says he doesn't have to. Says he's doing business with a new supplier, and he has no intention of honoring his past due invoices with us."

Rafe fell silent. In the icy compartment, his breath frosted the air. The anger that brewed within him, however, was red hot.

Tom, clearly agitated, rubbed his gloved palms together. "Someone is moving in on us, Rafe."

"Yes, dear," the viscount replied in a bored monotone. But, there was no mirth in his long-standing joke. He and Tom Wickham had been in business together so long that they thought of themselves as inextricably bound to one another. Now, the thought of that illicit union chafed Rafe's nerves. The thought of divorcing himself from Tom Wickham—and from the smuggling business—occupied an increasingly large portion of Rafe's mind. "The question is who?"

"If we don't find out quickly, we're going to be

broke. Whoever it is, he's telling our customers they don't have to pay us. He's underselling us and undercutting us. He's undermining our ability to stay in business!"

"Would that be so terrible, Tom?" Rafe watched his friend absorb this comment.

The younger man's expression changed from incredulity to disbelief in a matter of seconds. "Are you serious? What would we do?"

"We'd do what ordinary citizens do, Tom. We'd make an honest living."

Tom blanched. "But, how?"

"We could import something other than contraband liquor and wine. We could ship molasses and rum to and from the islands. We could take jobs in a bank if we had to."

"But a gentleman isn't supposed to work that hard, Rafe."

"We're not gentlemen, then, are we? Yes, I've got a title, but what good has that ever done me? Without the funds to back me up, I'm nothing but a genteel parvenu. But I have made money in the shipping business in the past, Tom. I know how to do it. I could do it again. Without trafficking in illegal goods."

"I don't know." Tom peered absently out the window. The scene outside was bleak, a littered alleyway running behind a row of chop houses, hotels, and taverns. The dimming rays of the late afternoon sun did little to brighten the dingy bricks, and much less to warm the Spartan interior of the coach. With a shiver, Tom murmured, "I don't know," and dipped his head.

"Are you—" Rafe clamped his lips shut. If Tom had a tear in his eye, it was because the idea of finding a new line of work, indeed, forging a new life, was altogether too frightening to imagine. Rafe was frightened by the notion, too. But he was more terrified by the idea of chasing debtors the rest of his life. He was weary of worrying about other smugglers cutting in on his territory. Being shot at had lost its excitement. And Rafe was tired of being ashamed of what he did.

"Sometimes change is good," he said quietly.

Chin to chest, Tom sniffed.

Exhaling a deep breath, Rafe reached up and knocked on the ceiling. When the hatch opened, he instructed the driver to head for home. The carriage bounced hard as it rolled over a deep rut and emerged from the alleyway into the bustle of Brighton's downtown traffic.

"Out of the way, man!" Rafe's driver made an abrupt turn at the corner, spooking his team of horses, and nearly tipping the carriage over. The coach skidded on two wheels, flinging Tom to the floor. Rafe grasped one of the leather straps that hung from the ceiling and managed to remain on the squabs, but when the rig righted itself, landing on all four wheels, the jolt was bone-shattering.

Horses hooves clattered on the cobblestones. Sliding toward the window, Rafe spied the figure of a black-clad horseman galloping past. After a few moments, when the horses had calmed, the driver had ceased yelling and the equipage had merged safely into traffic, Tom scrambled to his seat. The near miss with the speeding horseman had seemingly been as good as a mile, but both men stared at one another in open astonishment.

"What the bloody hell happened?" Tom cried.

"Someone cut in front of us. If it hadn't been for the quick actions of our driver, a man would be dead right now."

"That idiot on horseback nearly caused four deaths, including our driver's." Tom gently massaged the top of his head. He winced, then studied his fingertips as if expecting to see blood. "Did you get a look at him, Rafe?"

"I did." Reaching up, Rafe knocked on the ceiling door. When it opened, he had a brief conversation with the driver about the incident they'd just experienced. Then, he instructed the man to drive to Mrs. Simca's.

Tom gaped. "You must have had quite a bump on your head, too, if you want to go back there. What in the devil are you thinking?"

"I'm thinking that the man on horseback looked terribly familiar, Tom. And I've got a hunch Mrs. Simca knows him, too."

In the light of day, Mrs. Simca looked a decade older. Sitting in her small office, sipping tea, she looked more the aging dowager than the mistress of one of the finest and most exclusive brothels in England. She scrutinized Rafe as if she were studying a frame of needlepoint. "I'm afraid my client list is confidential, Lord Pershing."

Rafe smiled. "Mrs. Simca, let me explain something to you. A young lady in your employ has been brutally beaten. Someone took my snuffbox from her and returned it to me through an unwitting conduit. I believe this same individual made an attempt on my life. I want to know the name of that individual, Mrs. Simca, and I don't want to hear that his name was Mr. Brown."

"Who do you think it was, my lord? The man who beat up Baby called himself Mr. Brown. She gave you a description. Beyond that, I can't help you."

"You told me that in your line of business, it was important to know who you are dealing with."

Mrs. Simca's eyes narrowed. "That is true."

"What sort of background investigation did you conduct on Mr. Brown?"

"I cannot disclose that information."

Rafe leaned forward in his chair. "You told me before that the man had an impeccable reference. I want to know who that reference was, and I want to know now. Or else . . ."

"Or else what, my lord? Do you think for one moment that I would allow myself to be intimidated by you? My connections with the local authorities, as well as at Court, might surprise you. Don't threaten me. You will be sorry."

"I'm sorry I ever came here in the first place. I made a mistake, a mistake that could have cost Adelaide her life. Now, I am trying to rectify that mistake. And I will risk anything to do that, including my reputation and my wealth."

He saw her eyes widen. She was intelligent enough to realize that a man with nothing to lose was dangerous. In the elongated moment that followed, she considered her options. "If I tell you who referred Mr. Brown to me, what will you do?"

"If you don't tell me, I will burn this place to the ground," Rafe replied quietly.

Her gaze flickered. At length, she said, "He was referred here by Lord Toppainsley."

The pronouncement slammed into Rafe like a ton of bricks. Sliding back in his chair, he experienced a wave of queasiness. Disgust washed over him as the implications of Mrs. Simca's revelation unfolded. "Is he a regular customer of yours?"

She nodded.

"Was he here the night I met Adelaide?"

"She was sitting with him in the far corner when you entered the parlor. She excused herself, and left him to join you."

It pained Rafe to listen. "But, I didn't see Lord Toppainsley that night."

"The room is shadowy," Mrs. Simca replied. "For a reason."

"But a dandified relic like Lord Toppainsley would have been difficult to overlook. That powdered wig of his was out of fashion twenty years ago—"

"What powdered wig?"

Mrs. Simca's question raised the hair on Rafe's neck. Slowly, he stood, half aware of his surroundings. His head felt heavy and his mouth was cottony. The clue Mrs. Simca had dropped in his lap weighted him with fear.

* * *

Rosalind put as much distance between herself and her parents as possible the moment she stepped into the Toppainsley's glittering ballroom. Though this wasn't her first Toppainsley party, the opulent hall, heated to the point of suffocation by the volume of people it held, still stole her breath.

Mrs. Childress opened a pearl-embossed reticule and extracted her tiny flask. After quickly glancing around, she took a sip.

"Please, Mrs. C.! If Father sees you, he'll send us both home at once."

"If you're not worried about your father's admonitions, why should I be?"

Her governess had a point, but Rosalind was in no mood to debate it. Truth be told, she worried that Mrs. Childress drank too heavily; she didn't care a whit whether Sir Sibbald approved.

"I hope he doesn't make an appearance," Rosalind said, plucking two champagne flutes off a passing servant's silver tray.

Mrs. Childress accepted the proffered drink. "I don't suppose the 'he' you're referring to is Lord Pershing."

"He'd have no reason to attend."

"Except that he seems to be the Toppainsley's favored guest, of late."

Rosalind nibbled her lower lip. "Yes, that's quite strange, isn't it? Lord Toppainsley must want to purchase Lord Pershing's oceanfront property very badly. I suppose it has something to do with the ships he owns."

"Well, dearie, don't look now, but Viscount

Pershing just entered the room. With his faithful side-kick, Mr. Wickham."

He didn't see her at first. Rosalind watched him enter the room, shoot his cuffs and look around. His broad shoulders and handsome physique were arresting, drawing the stares of many ambitious mamas and their daughters. Even from halfway across the crowded ballroom, Rosalind could see the strong angle of his jaw, the somewhat arrogant tilt of his head. His thick black hair gleamed beneath the candlelight. The sight of his long, lean legs, shown off by black satin knee-pants, added an unbidden dollop of excitement to her already racing pulse.

"I've got to admit, he's a handsome man," Mrs. Childress said.

"He's not ugly," replied Rosalind tartly. She'd resolved not to let her emotions run away with her, particularly in regard to the viscount. She'd been silly to fall into his arms the night she met him, and more foolish still to allow him to kiss her during that now-infamous carriage ride home.

But, Lord Pershing was not the man for her. He'd said so himself, and Rosalind figured that he was in the best position to know. When he said he wasn't interested in knowing her, she took him at face value. She had too much pride to throw herself on a man who didn't like her. If Rafe Lawless didn't care for her, well, then, she cared even less for him.

All she needed from Lord Pershing was a bit of information concerning Redd Fellowes. Otherwise, he was of no interest to her.

"He's coming over here." Mrs. Childress took another sip of champagne. As Rafe and Tom approached, she said, "What exactly happened in the drawing room before I managed to escape that wicked Tom Wickham and burst down the doors?"

Turning her back to the advancing men, Rosalind smirked. Mrs. Childress didn't break down the doors, but it had sounded as if she were going to. By the time the governess entered, however, Rosalind had turned on her heel and was marching out. Mrs. Childress had been forced to abandon her siege against the viscount in order to follow Rosalind's hurried retreat.

"Nothing happened in the drawing room, Mrs. C. I merely attempted to convince the viscount he should tell me where Redd Fellowes is. He refused, scoundrel that he is. Really, I have nothing more to say to him."

"You'd better think of something," Mrs. Childress murmured.

"Good evening, Miss Yardley." The viscount's voice was as smooth as melted chocolate and just as tempting. "I didn't expect to find you here this evening."

She considered giving him the cut direct. But, as she sipped her champagne, Rosalind noted that the Lord and Lady Toppainsley were watching. She didn't want them to think her rude, particularly not when she planned to persuade Lord Toppainsley to tell her where Mr. Fellowes was.

She lifted her chin and looked at Rafe. "We seem to be on the Toppainsleys' short list when it comes to his favorite guests."

"Given the frequency with which the Toppainsleys

entertain, I suspect their list of favorite guests is quite lengthy," the viscount parried.

A strained but polite round of hellos took place between Tom and Mrs. Childress. Then, the foursome stood awkwardly, with Rafe and Rosalind exchanging looks as widely open to interpretation as an Egyptian scroll.

Lord Toppainsley, looking every bit the Sun King right down to his high-heeled shoes, joined the huddle. "I'm delighted that you accepted my invitation, Lord Pershing." He warmly greeted his other guests, but his focus was plainly on the viscount. "Have you given any more thought to selling your property?"

Pershing shook Toppainsley's hand, but his smile was bleak. "There's nothing to think about. I have no intention of selling out."

Topper's brows arched beneath his powdered wig. "Pity. It would save us all so much trouble."

"Precisely what do you mean?" Pershing asked.

"Oh, nothing." Gesturing toward the dance floor, Toppainsley said, "I do hope you and Miss Yardley will lead the waltz again. Your daring was the talk of the town last week! 'Twas one of our most successful parties ever!"

Rosalind wished she had one of those silly little fans most girls carried; a breeze across her clammy skin would have been welcome. "I'm afraid my waltzing days are over, my lord."

"As are mine," concurred Rafe.

"Too bad." Toppainsley struck a pensive pose. "I had thought you two made such a handsome couple. Lady Topper and I discussed it. I had even thought to put in a good word with Sir Sibbald. I know he's given you quite a rough go of it, Rafe. But, it's only natural. Rosalind is his only daughter, and since her mother's death, he's grown so over-protective. Keep at it old man, and you might turn him around yet.''

Indignation slammed against Rosalind's ribs. How dare this top-lofty fop interfere so boldly in her affairs? How dare he speak of her father so condescendingly? And of her as if she were a child?

She didn't realize her mouth was gaping until Mrs. Childress discreetly reached up and closed it. Eyes stinging, she looked at Rafe whose perturbation was equally evident. Embarrassed and humiliated, she couldn't decide who she was most angry with, Rafe, Topper or her father.

"I'm sure Sir Sibbald has his daughter's best interest at heart," Rafe said smoothly. "But, he is not the reason Rosalind and I are not waltzing this evening. Quite frankly, our decision whether to waltz is our own.''

At least the viscount had the backbone to defend himself against Topper's rudeness! Rosalind opened her mouth to speak, but Mrs. Childress's firm squeeze on her elbow was a reminder that she had manners and breeding and that stooping to Topper's level of misbehavior served no fitting purpose. Especially since she hadn't yet asked him about Redd Fellowes.

Clamping her lips shut, she met Rafe's gaze. Despite the anger Rosalind felt for him, she felt the intimacy of his gaze. He didn't like her, much less love her. He'd made that perfectly clear. He wouldn't be coerced or embarrassed into dancing with her. For that, she didn't blame him. But, at least he had the decency and the chivalry to put old Topper in his place. She thought if she hadn't fallen in love with him, she'd have liked him very much as a friend. Desperately, she wondered if that were still possible.

Her father's appearance couldn't have been more ill-timed. Sir Sibbald's salutations, particularly to Rafe, were brusque. Glancing around the room, Rosalind noticed that Dovie and Lady Toppainsley were in earnest conversation near the punch table. As if sensing someone's scrutiny, Dovie lifted her head, but when her gaze met Rosalind's, she looked away.

As it turned out, Dovie had been outside the study door when Rosalind and Sir Sibbald exchanged heated words. Since then, Dovie had scrupulously avoided Rosalind. It had been a tense twenty-four hours, but Rosalind had not apologized. She'd meant everything she'd said, after all, and, though it pained her to know she'd injured Dovie's feelings, she wouldn't lie and say she was sorry.

"Rosalind, I saw one of your chums from riding academy. Penelope Something-or-Other." Sir Sibbald gave her a pointed look. "Why don't you go and say hello to her."

"Alright, Father." Eager for an excuse to leave, Rosalind left the little group and, with Mrs. Childress at her side, searched in vain for a woman she hardly remembered meeting ten years earlier. "Father just wanted to get me away from Lord Pershing," she finally told her governess, exasperated.

Mrs. Childress nodded.

Standing beside the potted palms, Rosalind was unable to keep her eyes off Rafe. Her father had returned to Dovie's side near the punch table, where he conversed with her and Lady Toppainsley. Rafe and Tom Wickham were now in hot debate with Lord Toppainsley; Rosalind's distant observation was that the men appeared to be at odds about something.

"Come, Mrs. Childress, I am going to ask Lord Toppainsley if he knew where Redd Fellowes is."

"Oh, child, please don't! The men look monstrous angry. I don't think this is a good time—"

But if her governess wouldn't accompany her, Rosalind would simply go without her. Tracked incessantly by the gazes of Sir Sibbald, Lady Dovie, and Lady Toppainsley, Rosalind and Mrs. Childress circumnavigated the dance floor and stood beside Rafe and old Topper.

The men went strangely silent when the women materialized.

"Forgive me for interrupting, my lords." A case of butterflies was suddenly released in Rosalind's stomach. From the looks on the men's faces, she'd interrupted a much more heated argument than she'd guessed was taking place from across the room. Rafe's expression was stony. Topper's complexion was mottled. Both men stared at her as if she'd grown a horn on her head. Tom Wickham edged backward like a man retreating from a coiled serpent.

"Miss Yardley, would you excuse us, please?" Topper smiled like a cadaver. "Lord Pershing and I are discussing some important business. Nothing a young lady would be interested in."

"Oh, but I *am* interested." Rosalind batted her eyelashes, but the men were implacable, so she plowed forward. "Lord Toppainsley, I have been trying to locate an individual named Redd Fellowes. He's a seaman who was recently injured as a result of my negligence. I understand that he has gone to sea on one of your ships. *The Windsong,* I believe. I was wondering if you could assist me in finding his family."

Topper's eyes bulged, and the veins at his temples throbbed purple. "I don't know what sort of devilry you are about, girl, but you'd better watch yourself!"

For a moment, Rosalind's smile remained in place. As Topper's words sank in, her heart stopped and her throat constricted. The man who stared at her now, in his lacy cuffs and cravat, was deadly serious and lethally furious. Had they not been standing in a crowded ballroom, she thought he might physically attack her.

"I—I'm sorry, my lord. I didn't mean to overset you."

"You knew exactly what you were doing. Who are you in cahoots with, gel? Is it Pershing here?" Topper jerked his head toward the punch table on the opposite side of the room. "Or is it Sir Sibbald over there? Perhaps I was wrong about him. Perhaps he would stoop to using his daughter as means of obtaining information about me."

"I don't know what you're talking about!" A rush of panic seized Rosalind.

Mrs. Childress held her arm protectively. "That's

quite enough, my lord. I believe Miss Yardley will be going home now. Thank you very much for a fine party."

"On the contrary, ma'am." Lord Toppainsley smiled like a demented jack-o'-lantern. "I believe you and Miss Yardley will be staying with me for awhile. At least until I figure out what to do with you."

Rosalind shook her head, released Mrs. Childress's arm, and pivoted. Suddenly, she wanted nothing more than the comfort of her father's arms and the protection of his embrace.

But a serving man clad in gaudy livery blocked her path. Rosalind took a side-step, but the servant mirrored her movement. She took another, but he remained in front of her. Frightened, she peered over his shoulder, searching the room for her father. Sir Sibbald, having abandoned the punch table, danced with Lady Dovie on the far side of the room, his back to Rosalind's plight.

"Pratt, you rotten scoundrel, what the hell are you doing?" Rafe took a step forward, but drew up short when another serving man sidled up beside him and poked a pistol in his ribs.

Confused, Rosalind gave Rafe a questioning look. His gaze met hers, transmitting myriad emotions, but most of all, regret.

"Get out of my way!" Rosalind said to the servant hindering her escape. "I want my father!"

She gasped at the jab between her ribs. Looking down, she saw an identical snub-nosed pistol poised beneath the servant's champagne tray.

"Take them to the cellar," Lord Toppainsley told his servants.

"Go easy now," said the man named Pratt. "Walk slowly toward the potted palms. You'll see an arched exit that leads to a short corridor. We'll go down the steps to the cellar, all in a nice little row."

"Be a good girl, Rosalind," said Lord Toppainsley. "Or else my men will put a bullet in your father's head."

Stifling a sob, Rosalind turned and looked at Mrs. Childress. A pistol was unnecessary to coerce the woman to go along; her childhood governess had no intention of leaving her. Arm in arm, the women walked slowly toward the screen of potted palms. Behind walked Lord Pershing followed by the two servants with their pistols. It might have looked an odd procession if anyone were watching, but a lively country rill had most everyone on the dance floor.

As she stepped behind the row of potted palms, Rosalind's heart sank. She'd ruined everything, not just for herself, but for Rafe Lawless and her father, too. She wasn't quite certain why her mention of *The Windsong* provoked Lord Toppainsley's act of madness, but she knew her actions had set this tragedy in action.

She wished she'd never run away from her stepmother's silly bonfire party. She wished she'd never defied her father's wishes. Most of all, she wished she'd never kissed Lord Pershing.

Twelve

Head down, shoulders sagging, Rosalind headed toward the door Lord Toppainsley had indicated. A sense of failure and doom overwhelmed her. How could she have been so foolish?

A crash sounded from near the punch table. At first, Rosalind thought a hapless servant had dropped a tray of glasses. Then, pausing in her forced march, she realized the crash came from the orchestra section. Through the screen of palms, she barely made out the sight of a musician standing on his chair, banging his cymbals together as if his life depended on it.

The distraction startled her captors also. "What the hell . . ." Topper demanded angrily from the rear of the line.

At once, a figure crashed through the line of palms. A man stood on the podium where the cymbalist had been, yelling something about a shipwreck. A crack of gunfire sounded. The servant named Pratt scrambled past Rosalind and disappeared like a rat. Ladies screamed while the dancers dispersed in a confused riot.

A split second later, Rosalind was aware of Rafe at her side, his hand closed around her upper arm. It was Tom Wickham who had plunged through the row of palms. He stood over Rafe's captor who was writhing on the floor, a little hole blown out of the seat of his satin breeches. Rosalind saw him bend down and whisper something in the man's ear. The man shook his head. Then, Rafe pressed his pistol to the man's temple. The din on the dance floor drowned the servant's speech, but whatever Tom had asked of him, he suddenly seemed willing to answer.

"Are you alright?" Rafe asked.

His nearness drew gooseflesh to her bare shoulders and neck.

"What's that man shouting about?"

With Mrs. Childress, they traversed the row of palms and stood on the edge of the dance floor. The pistol crack had sent half the partygoers to the floor, and the others were nervously emptying the ballroom. A handful of brave men were attempting to calm the crowd and determine what happened.

"Quiet, please, everyone!" The man on the cymbalist's podium threw up his arms. At last, the babble in the ballroom subsided sufficiently for his voice to be heard. "There's been a shipwreck off the coast of Hastings. Near the land's point."

"Where the net houses are?" someone asked.

"That's right. Every able-bodied man who can swim or row a boat is needed for the rescue mission!"

The murmur in the ballroom rose to a crescendo. Then, as the news sank in, men began to gather their womenfolk and make for the exit. People swarmed out of the ballroom like bees disgorged from their hive.

Rosalind followed Rafe as he pushed through the current of people. Mrs. Childress and Tom were right behind.

"Excuse me, but do you know the name of the ship that is foundering?" Rafe asked the man as he stepped from the podium.

"It's *The Windsong.*"

The news was a dagger through Rosalind's heart. She glanced wildly around, but couldn't see her parents, or the Toppainsleys. The thought of Redd Fellowes drowning filled her with sadness. She had to do something to help him.

Tom knew a quick passage out of the ballroom. He led the way through a side door, then to Rafe's carriage which stood waiting on a dark cross street. Rosalind and Mrs. Childress were quickly assisted into the rig, then Rafe and Tom hopped in and sat on the squab opposite them. The horses went from standing still to a gallop in less than ten seconds, and Rosalind found herself bouncing painfully against her governess's side.

"You'll be delivered home first, then Tom and I will head to Hastings," Rafe said as the carriage rounded a corner on two wheels.

"No, I want to go to Hastings!"

Mrs. Childress and Rafe protested vehemently. "It's too dangerous, Rosalind. You see now what you've got yourself into. Your mention of *The Windsong* nearly got you killed."

"Take me to Hastings with you, or I'll tell my father you're a smuggler."

"If he doesn't know already, it's a miracle," Rafe shot back.

"I don't think he does," Tom interjected. "When Toppainsley's men apprehended you, they rounded up Sir Sibbald and Lady Dovie as well. A couple of dandified bruisers dressed up like servants were leading them toward Topper's study. No doubt they had pistols hidden beneath their cuffs as well."

Rosalind's chest spasmed. "Dear God! Where are they? Have they been hurt?"

"I'm sorry, but I lost track of them when the commotion about the shipwreck commenced."

"Christ on a raft, Tom! Why the bloody hell did you have to tell her that?"

"No need for obscenities," reminded Mrs. Childress.

In the flickering light provided by the outside lanterns, Rafe's expression turned to marble. A spark of indecision flashed in his eyes, then he abruptly reached up and knocked on the ceiling. The hatch opened, admitting a whoosh of cold air and the clatter of horses' hooves.

"Yes, m'lord?" the driver yelled down.

"Straight to Hastings," Rafe yelled back, then pulled the door shut and, as the carriage rocked sideways, fell heavily on the leather bench seat. "I can't very well return you to your father if I don't know where he is, can I?"

"He could be dead!" Rosalind's fear gave way to outright terror. The thought of losing her father was unspeakably frightening. She loved him, and he loved her. And she wanted nothing more than for the man to be alive and happy. She wondered suddenly why she'd ever begrudged him a day of happiness, why she'd ever voiced a single doubt or apprehension about his marriage to Lady Dovie. Dovie had, after all, returned a smile to his lips after Rosalind's mother died. Had she not come along, Sir Sibbald would have been a very lonely man.

"Your father's a very intelligent, resourceful man," Rafe said calmly. "I wouldn't underestimate his ability to outwit Toppainsley's henchmen."

"Neanderthals in tight pants, that's what they are," Tom added consolingly.

Rosalind nodded. She had to believe what Rafe and Tom were telling her. To believe otherwise was beyond her endurance.

The carriage made it to Hastings in record time, rumbling to a stop on the cliff overlooking the beach. Other carriages had already arrived from neighboring towns and villages, while horses stood tethered to the railing that bordered the steep drop-off to the sand below.

Rafe said, "Stay here," to Mrs. Childress and Rosalind as he and Tom leapt to the ground, but both women clambered out anyway.

The foursome rushed to the rough stone stairs leading to the beach. Below, men with torches and lanterns ran about shouting instructions and warnings. In the distance, beneath the illuminating glow of a full moon, a tall-masted ship hunkered in the white-capped ocean. "It isn't safe, Rosalind," Rafe warned, grasping her shoulders.

"I don't care." She wrenched free of his hold, and ran down the steps.

Running toward the water's edge, she quickly surveyed the scene. Men were pushing small wooden dinghies into the churning ocean, paddling toward the dark hulk on the moonlit horizon. With each minute, the silhouette of the ship sank deeper into the water. The shouts of men crying for help carried on the wind.

Her cape swirled around her as she ran toward a small dinghy being shoved to sea. A pair of men waded through frigid water, pushing the boat against the sand, aiming it for the sinking ship. In the confusion of the rescue attempt, the men failed to see Rosalind hop into the boat. When they heard Rafe's voice, however, they halted their efforts, turning to stare in slack-jawed amazement.

"Hey, get that lady outta my boat!" One of the men sloshed through the water toward the stern, an angry look in his eyes.

Rafe clambered into the boat, and sat on the hard plank bench opposite Rosalind. "Get out of this boat!" he demanded, his gaze fierce and slightly desperate.

"No! I've done Redd Fellowes enough damage. I won't sit idly by while he drowns!"

"I said, get her outta my boat!" The man leaned toward Rosalind, his hands outstretched as if he meant to lift her out himself.

In one fluid movement, Rafe stood and sucker-punched the man right between his eyes. Staggering back, the man made it to the beach where he fell in a heap. The other man who'd been helping launch the boat ran to his fallen friend. Rafe resumed his seat and leaned forward, reaching for Rosalind's hands and clasping them in his.

"You don't understand, Rosalind. You don't need to rescue Redd Fellowes."

"Yes, I do. I owe it to him. More importantly, I owe it to myself."

"To yourself?"

"There isn't time to explain, Rafe. Suffice to say, I'm making my own decisions now. And taking responsibility for my actions. I was wrong to defy Father merely for the sake of doing so. There's no glory in rebellion for rebellion's sake. But, I've got to do what's right for me, and if it pleases Daddy, fine. And if it doesn't, well, then, I hope he will love me enough to let me make my own mistakes. If he is still alive, that is!"

Withdrawing her hands, she searched frantically for the oars. Her fingers closed around the end of a wooden shaft, but Rafe wrestled it away from her. They struggled briefly for control of the oar, then Rafe overpowered her, flinging the paddle aside. Roughly, he grabbed her shoulders and gave her a little shake.

"There is no Redd Fellowes!" He held her at arm's length, his jaw clenched, his black eyes gleaming, every muscle in his body radiating tension.

Her teeth chattered, as much from shock as from cold. Slowly, the meaning of Rafe's words found purchase in her brain. "What do you mean, there is no Redd Fellowes?"

"I mean, you didn't really shoot anyone that night in my house. I told you that so you wouldn't tell your father where you'd been."

"You—you made it up?"

"I thought if you believed you'd shot someone, you'd want to cover up your own wrongdoing. If you thought you'd be in trouble, you'd keep your mouth closed."

Rosalind sank onto the hard wooden bench. Around her, a flotilla of small boats took to the water, while lantern beams scanned the ocean's surface, and a few of the strongest seaman who'd been able to swim made it ashore. Stunned, she stared at Rafe, a hundred emotions swirling inside her, each one struggling for preeminence.

At last, her wounded pride won out. "You must have thought me a terribly shallow person," she whispered. "You must have thought I had no concern for anyone but myself."

Loosening his grip on her, inhaling sharply like a man who'd been punched in the belly, he sat back. "I suppose that is precisely what I thought."

"You thought me a silly girl whose only ambition was to marry well and please my father."

He shut his eyes. "That's what I thought," he whispered.

"Look at me!" Rosalind's anger bubbled up, but she spoke in carefully measured tones. When he looked at her, she felt the power and depth of his emotion. A tear sparkled in his eye. They stared at one another for a moment before Rosalind reached down and picked up the oar. She handed it to Rafe. *"Start rowing,"* she said quietly.

She found another pair of oars, and just as she got them into place, the pair of men who'd attempted to launch the boat earlier, shoved it toward the water. One of them yelled, "Good riddance!"

Rafe hesitated, but did nothing to stop the boat from gliding into the open sea. "But, Rosalind, there is no Redd—"

"Yes, I know." She gripped the oars, bent her back and heaved her weight forward. "But there are many more men just like him out there, Rafe. And we can't sit by and let them drown while we discuss our own little problems, can we?"

A funny half-growl, half-laugh escaped his lips as he stared at her. Then, without dropping his oars, he leaned forward and kissed her hard on the lips. After that, he resumed his seat at the prow of the little boat and rowed hard, so hard that his face was soon bathed in perspiration. When the dinghy neared the wreckage site, he secured the paddles and threw off his heavy cloak. Two men swam desperately away from the sinking *Windsong.*

"Over here!" Rosalind yelled. She secured her oars, found a length of rope and threw it on the water.

One of the men clutched the rope so fiercely that she nearly toppled overboard. Rafe quickly grabbed her end of the rope and reeled the man in. He pulled both men over the side of the dinghy, and as they collapsed on the floor of the narrow boat, drenched and heaving from the seawater they'd ingested, he scrambled to his oars. "Row, Rosalind, row! We've got to get these men to dry land!"

Muscles Rosalind didn't know existed burned with fatigue. Her back felt like it was going to snap. Rosalind's teeth chattered uncontrollably, and the cold, wet wind that sliced through her body made her wince in agony. But determination gave her strength. Leaning into her oars, she pushed with all her strength. Having learned what she was capable of, she'd never doubt her own integrity again.

On the beach, the scene was total chaos. As soon as the dingy made it ashore, Rafe barked out orders to the men whose boat he'd commandeered. The rescued seamen were quickly laid on pallets, then carried to a waiting carriage that would whisk them to a surgeon's office in Hastings proper.

Rafe lifted Rosalind in his arms and stalked toward the stairwell leading to the cliff. Mrs. Childress met them at the bottom of the steps and threw a blanket over Rosalind. Seconds later, Rosalind was inside Rafe's carriage, dimly aware of his soothing voice and protective embrace. Her limbs felt frozen, and she couldn't wriggle her toes. A fuzzy, otherworldly sensation enveloped her, and she struggled against the urge to fall asleep. The voices that surrounded her grew faint, until at last, she slipped into total blackness.

When she awoke, she was in an unfamiliar setting, propped against a bank of pillows in a room filled with worried whispers and shifting shadows. As if swimming through a murky fog, she fought to focus on the faces staring down at her. Their expressions of concern were unfamiliar to her; she had no idea who they were.

A wave of panic struck her, and she pushed herself to her elbows. An older man, broad-shouldered and gray-haired, gently pushed her back down. As she stared at him, her memory slowly faded back. That was Father sitting on the edge of her bed, staring down at her, his gaze full of hurt. And behind him hovered Lady Dovie, her eyes swollen, her hands wringing a limp kerchief.

Rosalind turned her head. Mrs. Childress stood on the other side of the bed, sniffling and sipping openly from a flask. Beside the governess stood Rafe Lawless, Viscount Pershing. And at the foot of the bed was Tom Wickham, his blond curls a frizzy tangle.

The roaring in her head receded as her father's muted voice took on clarity. "How do you feel, Rosalind?"

"Like I swam the Channel." She managed a small smile, eager to dispel the concerns of her friends and family. Her gaze slid to Lady Dovie's, and hot tears stung her eyes. "I'm sorry," Rosalind whispered.

Dovie, apparently rendered speechless with emotion, smiled through her own tears.

Sir Sibbald looked from his daughter to his wife. "You hadn't any business being in that boat, Rosie—"

Rosalind had enough strength to lay a fingertip on her father's lips. "I hadn't any business questioning your right to marry Dovie, Father. I hadn't any business interfering in your life, or trying to keep you all for myself. But, I had every right and privilege to join in the rescue effort. Are the two men we rowed to shore alright?"

Tom Wickham answered that question. "Right as rain, Miss Yardley. They were tough old salts, I assure you. A few minutes in the ocean didn't cause them any permanent injury."

She looked at Rafe. Her father followed the trajectory of her gaze, and said, "I ought to call you out for allowing my daughter to get in that boat. She could have fallen overboard and drowned. She could have frozen to death. At the very least, you should have thought of the propriety of allowing a single woman to witness such violent carnage."

Rosalind started to defend Rafe's actions, but changed her mind. The viscount was perfectly capable of standing up to her father's challenge.

"Your daughter has a mind of her own, Sir Sibbald. I'm afraid when she gets an idea in her head, there's no talking her out of it."

"Poppycock! She's a young girl. She needs protection!"

"I beg to differ, sir," Rafe said smoothly. "She's shown her mettle, and she's quite capable of taking care of her herself."

"I'll drink to that," Mrs. Childress chortled.

As her strength returned, so did Rosalind's recollection of the events leading up to the shipwreck. "Father, how did you and Dovie escape Toppainsley's henchmen?"

Balefully, Sir Sibbald jerked his chin in Dovie's direction. "You tell her, dear." He drew one hand down his face, smearing an exasperated frown onto his features. "My god, it seems the women are taking over."

"When the great crash sounded in the ballroom, our captors were momentarily distracted. They hesitated, looked at one another, then looked over their shoulders. I took the opportunity to withdraw a hatpin from my reticule. I always keep one pinned to the lining, you know, in the event that the wind picks up, or the elements—"

"Yes, yes," Sir Sibbald interrupted. "At any rate, she gouged one man in his private parts, causing him to drop his pistol. That gave me time to grab the other fellow's pistol. We managed to make a clean escape after that. We fought the flow of traffic streaming from the ballroom, but by then you'd already left with Lord Pershing. The man who announced the wreck saw you leave. So, we hopped in our carriage and made our way to Hastings, knowing, of course, that Lord Pershing would go straight there."

"I don't know why you'd assume such a thing," Rafe said.

"Because I know what you do for a living," Sir Sibbald snapped.

Suppressed hostility shrouded the room. For a few moments, no one said a word. Then, Rafe, his backbone stiff and his gaze level, broke the silence. "I suppose Lord Toppainsley informed you."

"Lady Topper, actually."

"She's a terrible gossip," inserted Lady Dovie nervously. "I suppose she could have been lying, Sibbald."

"Was she, Rafe?" Sir Sibbald asked him.

"No." He took a deep breath and looked at Rosalind. "She told you the truth, part of it, at least. What she didn't tell you was that her husband has been trying to run me out of business these last few weeks."

When Lady Dovie gasped, Rafe allowed himself a slight, wry smirk. He glanced at Tom's dazed expression, regretting that his confession would ultimately implicate his friend in criminal activities. He'd do his best to exonerate Tom, but, in the end, they would both be responsible for their actions.

"Sorry, Tom," he said quietly.

To his surprise, Tom replied, "It's actually quite a relief, isn't it, dear?"

The men exchanged a chuckle over their private joke while Sir Sibbald looked even more confused. Rosalind punched up a bolster behind her head, and sat up. Mrs. Childress sank onto the edge of the bed and continued drinking, while Lady Dovie laid a comforting—*or was it a restraining?*—hand on her husband's shoulder.

"We first knew someone was cutting in our territory when our customers began refusing to pay. One of them actually shot at us, apparently convinced that his new supplier would support and defend such violence."

Tom interrupted. "Toppainsley may even have paid Mr. Sawyer to kill us. But it was Pratt who told Toppainsley we were heading toward The Cockeyed Rooster that night. It all made sense the moment I saw Pratt parading around Toppainsley's ballroom in that frilly French costume."

Nodding, Rafe crossed his arms over his chest. "Pratt was Toppainsley's spy. And it was Pratt who shot at us as we entered Toppainsley's town house. It was Pratt who slipped the poison in Rosalind's drink. Unfortunately, for Mrs. Childress, she got the vile stuff that was intended for Rosalind. His job was to get rid of me and Rosalind, too, but he kept missing his mark. Of course, I didn't piece the puzzle together until after I visited Mrs. Simca's in Brighton."

"Mrs. Simca's?" Sir Sibbald stood abruptly, jostling Rosalind's neat little mountain of pillows. He jerked his arm from Dovie's grasp and shook his fist at Rafe. "How dare you mention such a place in front of my daughter? I knew you were a good-for-nothing—"

"Your daughter's old enough to hear this story!" Rafe's voice boomed, then, when Sibbald shrugged and shook his head, he resumed his normal tone of voice. "And you, sir, might as well hear my complete confession now. You'll hear it at trial, I suppose. You and everyone else in this room. I did nothing at Mrs. Simca's that I'm ashamed of, nothing at all."

Sir Sibbald scoffed.

"Admittedly, my intentions might have been different when I entered the place, but—" Rafe gestured helplessly with his hand. The truth was, he went to Mrs. Simca's to rid himself of the physical agony Rosalind had put him in. When he realized that his desire for her completely eclipsed his desire for anyone else, he merely talked to Adelaide, putting the unfortunate woman in harm's way, a situation he deeply regretted.

Pinching the bridge of his nose, Rafe concluded that portion of his confession could wait until a solicitor was retained. If he told it now, Sir Sibbald might be driven to commit murder. "You'll have to take my word, Sir Sibbald. I did not employ the services of any of the women at Mrs. Simca's. Nevertheless, I lost my silver snuff box there."

"The one I found in my muff?" Rosalind asked.

"Lord or Lady Toppainsley must have put it there," Rafe said. "They knew you would return it to me. It was a message to me, letting me know that every move I made was being watched."

Gaze narrowed, Sir Sibbald asked, "So how did Toppainsley find the silver snuff box? Was he at Mrs. Simca's, too, that evening?"

"Yes, and for all I know, he was sitting right beside me. He wasn't wearing his powdered wig, you see."

"And it was Toppainsley who fired off a shot at us in Brighton, just yesterday, when we were attempting to collect another bill," Tom said.

"Quite right. But it was Pratt who injured our friend Adelaide and actually stole the box from her. I'm afraid Pratt did most of Topper's dirty work, even while working under our employ."

"I'd like to get my hands on him," Tom said.

"No, no! It's just too fantastic!" cried Sir Sibbald. "Why would a man like Toppainsley, wealthy beyond imagination, want to take over your smuggling operation?"

"How do you think he got so rich, sir? Just because

a man's got a title doesn't mean he's got a ton of money. Toppainsley's been in the shipping business for years, and so's his family. Too proud to admit it, but he's trafficked in everything from slaves to sugar. Hardly a noble profession, not the way he's carried it on, I assure you."

Rosalind stirred amidst her pillows. "Is that why Topper got so angry when I mentioned his ship *The Windsong*?"

Rafe stared at her. With her damp hair strewn across the pillows, she was the prettiest thing he'd ever seen. *And the bravest, and the most willful.* If he'd ever thought her a spoiled child, he certainly didn't regard her that way now.

He shook himself out of his reverie to answer her question. "When you mentioned *The Windsong*, Toppainsley thought you were passing along a warning, either from me or from your father. He thought his scheme to get rid of me and take over my territory had been found out. You see, very few people were aware he owned that ship—"

"But, Lady Toppainsley told me!" Rosalind looked at Dovie. "You heard her!"

"Yes, and she was in her cups that night," Dovie murmured.

"The evils of alcohol!" Sir Sibbald proclaimed, pointing his finger to the ceiling.

Dovie shook her head, and touched her husband's arm. "Darling, you like a drink now and then as much as anyone."

"Here, sir, have a snort," Mrs. Childress offered.

Sir Sibbald's jaw fell slack, then his face turned

scarlet, then his entire body shook like a dog when it throws off water. He seemed to be undergoing some sort of catharsis, or spiritual trial by fire. When he was still, his expression was one of world-weary resignation. He was a man whose ordered existence had turned topsy-turvy, yet he was struggling mightily to make sense of what had happened to him in the last few days.

The silence stretched thinner and thinner. Then, everyone watched in startled sympathy as Mrs. Childress reached across the bed, and Sibbald, with a heavy sigh, took the proffered flask from her fingers. With a quick jerk, he threw back his head and drank long.

"That's enough, dear." Dovie took the flask from his lips, helped herself to a sip and passed it back to Mrs. Childress. With a shudder and a sigh, she said, "Everybody needs a little nip once in a while."

If Rafe hadn't been so aware that his entire life was hanging in the balance, he might have laughed. Rosalind chuckled happily, and to his surprise, reached out and squeezed Dovie's hand. The atmosphere in the room was warming, particularly within the confines of the Yardley family, but the fact remained that Rafe had just confessed to a capital crime and if Sir Sibbald carried out the duties of his office, the result would be transportation to Australia . . . or hanging.

"Well, that's just about the sum total of it," Rafe said. "If you wouldn't mind, sir, I'd like to have a private word with your daughter. After that, I will submit to your custody."

Sibbald balked at leaving his daughter alone with an admitted smuggler, but Dovie tugged on his sleeve. "We'll be right downstairs," she reminded him. "They can't elope in five minutes, now can they?"

"Knowing them, they'll climb out the window and high-tail it to Gretna Green!" But, in the end, Sibbald yielded to his wife's entreaties, and left the room with everyone else. "Five minutes," he said over his shoulder as he crossed the threshold. "After that, I'm clamping you in hand-shackles!"

When the door closed behind them, Rafe moved around the bed and sat on the edge of the mattress. There was little time to explain himself to Rosalind, and her sweet, glowing expression, so tantalizing and so tempting, confused his efforts to find the right words. He had so much to tell her, about his life with Annette, about his previous failings, about his ill-fated decision to enter the smuggling business. But, when she reached out from beneath her covers and laid her hands atop his, he could only say one thing.

"I love you, Rosalind."

Her lips curved. "I know."

Fighting back a wall of tears, he managed a dry chuckle. "Had things been different, had I not been in this despicable trade, do you think you might have loved me, Rosalind?"

"I think I love you now, Rafe."

His heart twisted. The words he wanted to hear so badly were bittersweet now that he was going to be transported . . . or hung.

He drew her hand to his cheek. "I'm so sorry. So sorry."

"Don't be, Rafe. Whatever happens, I want to be with you."

"Darling, you can't know what you're saying—"

She pressed a fingertip to his lips. "Shush. Haven't we spent the last few days establishing that I am perfectly capable of making my own decisions? Don't patronize me now, Rafe. If I say I want to be with you, who are you to contradict me?"

"We can never be together, Rosalind. If I'm lucky, I'll spend the remainder of my life in Australia—"

"I've never been there. I hear the weather's nice."

"There's no life for you there, Rosalind. Without your friends and family—"

"Mrs. C. will go with us. Father and Dovie can visit."

He wanted her so badly his body ached. Leaning down, he buried his head in the crook of her neck, allowing her to stroke his head and whisper soothing words in his ear. Her breath was cool and sweet upon his neck, her touch comforting, arousing, and seductively familiar. The thought of making love to her was too painful, and too exquisite, to imagine.

His life flashed before his eyes. It was a panorama of risk and regret. He thought if he could have changed the course of his life, he would have never embarked on a criminal career, an endeavor that ultimately alienated him from the woman he loved. But, regrets were for poets, and reality was unalterable. Kissing Rosalind softly on her lips, Rafe indulged his own last wish.

But when she laced her arms around his back, he resisted her embrace. Straightening, he pulled away from her. Her lips were slightly parted and her eyes glazed with desire. Leaving Rosalind Yardley in that room, and walking downstairs to turn himself in to her father, was the most gut-wrenching thing Rafe Lawless had ever done.

Thirteen

Rafe paused at the landing, composing himself, tamping down the unmasculine tears that threatened to spill from his eyes. In his emotional state, he considered stalking back into his bedroom, gathering Rosalind up in his arms and doing precisely what Sibbald had predicted, escaping out the window and eloping to Gretna Green. But, if Rosalind Yardley could assume responsibility for her actions, so could he. Gripping the stair rail, he knew what he had to do.

Before he took a step, the familiar brogue of Cyril Crawley filtered up from his drawing room. Unable to make out Crawley's words, Rafe froze. Tom Wickham's voice as well as Sir Sibbald's mingled in angry, defensive tones. Pricking his ears, Rafe strained to hear, but the creaking of the house overrode Crawley's voice.

Crawley had no business in his house; he'd never been there before. There was something about the situation that caused Rafe's nape to prickle and his heart to race. The addition of Toppainsley's affected speech made his stomach turn.

Tom's voice rose to an alarmingly shrill pitch. "You won't take him. He's barricaded himself in the cellar. You can't get in!"

Rafe half leaned over the banister to hear Crawley's response. "I've got men surrounding this place. He can't get out alive, Tom."

Realization slammed into Rafe like a runaway mail coach. Rafe and Tom routinely locked the cellar door from the inside so that curious chambermaids and cooks couldn't wander down there. Apparently, Crawley, having tried the door, concluded Rafe was holed up in there. That's why Crawley hadn't searched the upstairs of Rafe's house. That's why Crawley was certain Rafe would make a dash for safety out the back door of his cellar.

Tom's unnaturally loud voice was meant to be heard. "Killing us won't do you any good, Topper. Even if you get rid of Sir Sibbald, the law will track you down. You might as well untie us, and turn yourself in. Add murder to your slate of crimes, and you'll wind up dancing in the wind!"

"Shut up, you little fool, or you'll be choking on your cravat!"

"You're an evil man," Dovie cried.

The loud crack that followed told Rafe she was rewarded for her outburst with a slap across the face. Rage coursed through his veins, but his thinking was clear and focused.

A muffled conversation ensued between Toppainsley and Crawley. Rafe deduced that the men had surprised Tom, Sir Sibbald and the women when they came downstairs. If Crawley and Toppainsley were armed with pistols, they'd have had little difficulty in tying up the foursome. The question now was how to free the captives without getting them shot into the bargain.

Rafe removed the pistol he always kept tucked in his front waistband. He stepped out of his dancing slippers, and moved stealthily down the stairs, weapon poised at the ready.

Halfway down the staircase he stepped on a creaky board. Holding his breath, he froze. But, Crawley and Toppainsley had commenced arguing, and as their voices grew louder, Rafe moved more quickly down the steps.

"Go and see for yourself!" Crawley exclaimed. "The door is impenetrable, I tell you!"

Toppainsley blasted his accomplice. "Fool! You should have lured Pershing into the drawing room before you showed your pistol! He must have heard you, then scampered back into his hole like a rat!"

"You're the one who pulled out your pistol first! I was sitting here playing the pretty with the four of them when you barged in, raving like a lunatic. I had no choice then, did I, but to threaten to shoot the women if the men didn't cooperate!"

"Blast it all to hell!" Toppainsley's high-heeled shoes stomped across the carpet. "Stay here, then. I'll fetch Pratt from outside, and we'll blow the cellar door off with gunpowder if we have to!"

Toppainsley's footsteps neared the open door of the drawing room. In a second, he would emerge onto the landing. Rafe would be in full view, then, and well within range of Toppainsley's pistol. If Toppainsley killed Rafe, there would be no one left to protect Sir Sibbald, Dovie, Mrs. C. and Tom.

Like a panther, Rafe moved down the remaining two steps. As he made the landing, Toppainsley strode angrily out of the drawing room. There was a split second in which the two men locked gazes. Toppainsley's eyes lit on Rafe's pistol. Comprehension widened his eyes, and his own pistol came up, but too late . . .

The crack of gunfire was deafening. Rafe leapt over Toppainsley's crumpled body and rushed into the drawing room. Scanning the darkened chamber, he saw the captives seated side by side on the sofa, Sir Sibbald and Tom bookends to the women, all of their ankles and wrists bound with sailor's rope. Standing beside the sofa, his arm outstretched, a pistol clutched in his hand, was a startled Cyril Crawley.

The nose of Crawley's pistol swung in a wide arc and came to rest a hair's breadth from Sir Sibbald's temple. "Drop your weapon, Rafe, or I'll shoot."

"I should have known you would play the middle, Cyril." The pistol fell from Rafe's fingers, landing on the carpet with a soft thud.

"Toppainsley wanted to move in. He offered me a better deal, Rafe. Business is business, old man. You should understand that."

"I understand you are a piece of stinking offal," Rafe replied, moving closer to the sofa. Unarmed, he was no threat to Cyril. The underpaid shore guard seemed to actually enjoy this opportunity to lord it over Rafe. "I'll bet you couldn't wait to tell Toppainsley that Rosalind had wandered into that cavern the night of the bonfires."

"He thought it hilariously funny. One way to get rid of Pershing, he said, was to turn Sir Sibbald against him. Aside from being a smuggler, the very worst thing a man could do was show some interest in Sibbald's daughter!" Crawley, thoroughly amused, laughed heartily.

Rafe took a step closer. Crawley's smile vanished, and he pushed his pistol deep into Sibbald's ear. To Sir Sibbald's credit, he remained still as a statue, his gazed fixed on Rafe, his expression entirely calm.

A creak sounded in a floorboard on the landing behind Rafe. Sir Sibbald's gaze flickered, then widened.

"Daddy?" Rosalind's voice raised the stakes. "Daddy, are you alright?"

"Saucy wench," muttered Crawley, licking his lips. His pistol wavered, then left Sibbald's temple and pointed at Rafe's heart. "Back up, man!" he hissed. In a louder voice, he called out, "Your father's fine, Miss Yardley. Lord Toppainsley won't be causing him any more trouble, as you can see! We're in the drawing room, dear, come in!"

"No!" screamed Dovie.

"Rosalind, run!" Sir Sibbald cried.

Rafe took one step backward as Crawley moved away from the sofa. Then, in the instant that followed, Rosalind's silhouette darkened the open drawing-room doors, and Crawley's head turned toward her. Rafe snatched the pistol he always kept tucked in the back waistband of his breeches, and fired.

The big man fell to the floor with a thunderous racket. Rafe whirled just in time to see Jemmy Pratt approach Rosalind from behind, encircling her body with his thick, muscled arm, and clamping his hand over her mouth. The pistol he held to Rosalind's head was the one he'd picked off Toppainsley's dead body.

Fury burned in Rafe's heart. He watched in horror as Rosalind's gaze rounded and locked with his. The fear in her eyes pained him more than the thought of his own hanging; he simply would not allow Pratt, or any other man, to injure his Rosalind.

"Let her go, Pratt, she's of no use to you."

"You told me she was dead!"

"I wanted you to forget about her. I wanted her to be safe!"

"Well, she ain't safe now!" Pratt nervously waggled the gun at the side of Rosalind's head. He was a two-bit sharpster who needed someone to tell him what to do, especially in the heat of a crime. With Toppainsley and Crawley apparently dead, his courage flagged and indecision assailed him.

"Put the gun down, Pratt. You don't want to hang for shooting that girl!"

"I'm already in a heap of trouble!" His voice broke as his gaze swept from Toppainsley to Crawley to the row of captives seated on the sofa, staring at him in open-mouthed terror.

"If you harm a hair on her head, Pratt," Rafe growled, "I will kill you, and it will be a slow, painful death. Injure her, and I have nothing left to lose. Do you know how dangerous a desperate man can be, Pratt?"

An unearthly groan escaped Toppainsley's body. The powdered wig moved and the satin-sheathed limbs shifted on the floor beside Pratt's feet. Pratt glanced down; Toppainsley's long, white fingers closed around his ankles.

"Sweet Jesus!" Pratt yelled, aiming his gun at Toppainsley and loosening his hold on Rosalind.

In the space of a heartbeat, Rafe leapt between Pratt and Rosalind.

Pratt's gun swung around again, discharging. The men fell to the floor, rolling on top of one another. Rosalind screamed, then ran into the drawing room, where she flung herself on her father's lap. Only after she'd hugged her father tightly, and made him promise not to send Rafe to Australia, did she agree to go to the kitchen, find a sharp knife, and cut the ropes that bound the prisoners' feet and wrists.

The wedding took place in Gretna Green, after all. With Sir Sibbald's blessing, the formalities of announcements and posting banns were dispensed with. His daughter was, after all, so eager to be married to Viscount Pershing, he didn't entirely trust that she would save her virginity for him if she had to wait another fortnight.

They wanted to spend their first married night in Rafe's house. A storm roared in from the ocean just as he moved inside her the very first time. Rosalind clung to Rafe as if her very soul had melted into his. The old house on the cliff creaked and moaned as it never had, but the walls remained strong and the roof kept the rain off its occupants' heads. The cellar offered up its finest champagne, while outside the waves lashed against the stony sheer.

When they were sated, Rafe lay on his back, Rosalind's head on his shoulder, her arm tossed over his chest. She toyed with the thick black hair that blanketed his chest. She loved every inch of his body and every nuance of his character.

"I still can't believe your father arranged for my pardon." Rafe, inhaling the scent of her hair, experienced the intoxication of complete satisfaction.

"Daddy wants me to be happy, Rafe. Just like I want him to be."

Chuckling, Rafe kissed the top of her head. "You really are accustomed to getting what you want, aren't you, dear, dear, Rosie?"

She smiled contentedly. "I only want you, dear. Only you."

More Zebra Regency Romances